Mystic Creek

Chris Phillips

PublishAmerica
Baltimore

ISBN: 978-1-61546-447-0 (softcover)
ISBN: 978-1-4489-1435-7 (hardcover)
PUBLISHED BY PUBLISHAMERICA, LLLP
www.publishamerica.com
Baltimore

Printed in the United States of America

To Stephanie Wright, who helped me believe that water could become wine;
Gabrielle Mokry who let the water touch the horizon…; and to the four little
girls who took the wrong turn on Lennox Lane…Rest in Peace…

XII / XII / MMIII

But most of all to you, the reader, to which I owe this dream…

To the Holts,
Thanks for the Support
Hope you enjoy
~ Chino Phillips

The Reaper and Flowers

There is a Reaper, whose name is Death,
And, with his sickle keen,
He reaps the bearded grain at a breath,
And the flowers that grow between.

"Shall I have naught that is fair?" Saith he;
"Having naught but the bearded grain?
Though the breath of these flowers is sweet to me,
I will give them all back again,"

He gazed at the flowers with tearful eye,
He kissed their drooping leaves;
It was for the Lord of Paradise
He bound them in his sheaves.

"My Lord has need of these flowerets gay,"
The Reaper said, and smiled:
"Dear tokens of the earth are they,
Where he was once a child."

"They shall all bloom in fields of light,
Transplanted by my care,
And saints, upon their garments white,
These sacred blossoms wear."

And the mother gave, in tears and pain,
The flowers she most did love:
She knew she should find them all again
In the fields of light above.

O, not in cruelty, not in wrath,
The Reaper came that day;
'Twas an angel visited the green earth,
And took the flowers away.

—Henry Wadsworth Longfellow 19th century poet

The Beginning...

A tall dark haired man sat at Tropicana Bar in the southern Zihuatanejo looking out on to the Pacific Ocean from the small bay the city was located in. At sunset the sky looked as though it were on fire, and the water was a smooth calm flowing glass which echoed softly in the distance as the waves came in slowly. The tide was changing. It was a calm and peaceful sight that blended well with the slow dancing rhythms coming from the bar out on to the sand where old couples stood dancing by the light of the sunset. In the tall man's hand was a bound section of papers, most of which had pencil scribbled all over them in a small cursive that was neat and precise but at the same time completely illegible. In his offhand he held a cigar traveling case made of polished ebony. The look made him seem like a mildly puzzled Cuban tourist, but then again the Tropicana was not a place where those who were perfect went. It was a small bar, with one foot in the sand and a view of the ocean, it relied mainly on various customers coming off the beach, rather than the greatest collection of drinks or entertainment. For a warm afternoon they were doing good, but the local crowd were taking their mid day siestas.

In one corner sat a gentleman sipping on a martini, reading over a copy of the New Yorker. Upon seeing the tall dark haired man, he smiled and put down the magazine.

"So my friend why this place, this bar isn't exactly that great of a location. It's well off the beaten path and I get the feeling that there isn't exactly the most *English oriented* people. There are so many better places that you could launch this." He said with a slight tone of annoyance that superiors many times had.

"As my editor I figured you would say that. I'm not looking for people who can understand these words, but for people who can understand what these feelings are. The salt of the earth, George. They'll be able to understand this no problem."

"I take it you'll be reciting this *fantasy* in Spanish then?" The publicist asked this time in an even more annoyed voice. The dark haired man sat down in the comfortable chair, and prepared everything, completely un-phased by the attention that he was drawing from the patrons who had been enjoying their drinks.

The tall dark man stopped a waiter and asked in fairly good Spanish, "Por favor un botella de gin. Y dos vasos tambien, gracias."

The waiter quickly went to the bar and the publicist stared at him with a blank stare of amazement that was clearly not accustomed to a man of his stature.

"Fine I'll get a translator to see if there's a way to listen to this in English. There's no way I'm going back to management with something that I tried to translate. By the way, Gin?" He said looking mildly disgusted, "I do vodka martinis."

"I forgot that you were a vodka man, but beggars can't be choosers, and I have no intention of telling this in another language. I learned Spanish in high school, and haven't used much of it since. The story, by the way, is not the one that you believe it to be. This is a story of a good friend of mine, on a very strange day back so many years ago."

"This isn't about *her* is it." The man said pointing at a very old photo that seemed to be used as a bookmark in the mess of papers assembled as a book.

The dark man lit a match in the motionless air, and then lit up a large cigar and puffed out the smoke, "Ahh...this story does involve her." He said looking into the faded photograph and smiling faintly before blowing out another puff from his cigar slowly closing his eyes, "Now if you would like to listen you are welcome to. This will be the last book that I will ever write."

"Knowing you I doubt that. Unless you finally saw a shrink and got yourself some Prozac or something." He said shaking his head and pouring himself a reasonable measure of gin.

"You know I won't ever touch that stuff." The author said pouring a generous measure himself. "This stuff is way cheaper." He joked, taking a smell of the auroma of juniper berries and citrus.

"Then the pages go blank forever..." The editor said slightly in the tone of a question, and slightly like a statement, but showing no abash he dug through his pocket pulling out a cigar encased in a fine glass tube.

"Enjoy it my friend this is a Cuban." Said the author, handing him a cigar out of the traveling humidor.

"So are these." The publicist said breaking the tube end open and pulling it out, with a little smile on his face.

"Mexico mi amigo, no es Cuba." He said puffing out a large amount of smoke.

"I'll take that to be some sort of insult in Spanish. Now are we just going to sit here all night and smoke or are you going to finally read that manuscript?"

The author just laughed, "I see no problem doing both...but if you insist...so it begins..."

Then he opened the book. There were plenty of typed words and scribbles from a black pen with comments all over the page. It seemed to be a largely re-written version of a book manuscript. As he prepared a few people came into the bar to sit down and hear the author who had no name, read the book that had never been published. There was something special about the atmosphere there, and from the beginning the words seemed to feel rather than heard. He began to read and a few people listened in behind the wall of smoke.

Chapter One
The Lives of the Dead

One of my favorite ironies that I love to quote is how that day began for Johnny. It was actually the night before that day in the small town of Elysium, Colorado. Elysium was a small town tucked away in the mountains. From all directions they seemed to fortify the small town with a lonely little highway extending down a place known as Blackstone ridge towards the outcrops of suburban Denver. Most of the folks in Elysium were used to the town. They had great pride in the small town. Lots of small owned businesses, lots of logos from the Elysium High School *Warriors* posted throughout the town. Epically since that last season as I recall they went to the semi-finals of State with star line-backer Theo Sandburg. At a small lonely house a father sat watching the late night shows on prime time TV wondering about the divorce, wondering about why it was that he was still there, and not off chasing the next dream. He cracked open another beer to join the growing collection at his feet.

One more drink and I'll move on…

Upstairs Johnny sat under a small lamp at a messy desk with a pencil in hand, as always writing. The alarm clock on the other side of the desk showed a bright red 3:00. In my memories of Johnny, I always remember how tired he was before that day. He always had his eyes glazed over, and when you asked him what time it was that he went to bed…2…6…it didn't matter. I would like to say that Johnny feared the dark; I'd like to say that I wanted to drug him so that he would sleep a dreamless sleep

11

for the rest of his life. That at least would be merciful. I think it was less cruel for him to grudge around lethargically, than it was to tell him to go to bed.

Johnny had a gift when it came to writing. I'd expect that if it weren't for that day…I think he could've made one of the best writers, and died a very miserable lonely death. He'd have been remembered by everyone, he'd have a day all to himself in Elysium, but paradise for some would have come at the cost of Hell for him.

And thank God that didn't happen…as ironic as it sounds…

He once told me it was the flow of things perhaps, maybe even his writing ability, maybe his need to express himself that told him that night to sit down and write, I don't think he really knew. It had always been something that he liked to do, but lately it was all that he could do. Somehow, the pencil started to carve away a story, a story just like his life, except nothing to do with him, it was about a queen on a far away frozen planet called Delthamar. One of the claims of critics against science fiction writers is that it can't relate to human emotion. I can't call what Johnny wrote literature but I can call it a lot more human than the tales of the Bard, and the writings of classics. They don't tell how it feels because they were written about beautiful things; beautiful topics of love, romance, and bravery, things that are romanticized in our culture as the beauty in life.

And life, to those like Johnny, is almost never beautiful.

Blood thinly carved away against the flesh of the page as Johnny's hand began to cramp as he started his thirteenth page for the night, for it was so much of him that he always put into his stories. They were his way of living again. They were his way of making everyone else around him alive and well again. But the more that ended up on the page the more that the paper resembled his soul, twisted and confused for an ending…scarred and torn. I have to imagine the page hurt as bad as he did inside. Numb pain that no one else around him seemed to feel. Numb pain that shattered the mind and crippled the soul and twisted it like crumpled paper. Eraser marks across the page were as clear as the scars across his body, both showing the horrors of the past.

The ending was in sight as Johnny wrote the last few lines. They were beautiful, but they weren't him…they sounded good and many people would have said that they fit, but they felt like a mismatching whites on a bright day. It stood there for almost an hour, the queen asking of her servant why it was that people died. But in the end the author had no more answers than the character, and both were hurting inside. So Johnny packed up at 4:00 in the morning to go to bed. That next day, he decided, he was going to stay home and skip school. He was just too stressed out; he just needed a break, needed to take the edge off of this sharp pain in his heart. He needed to fill the void that was sucking away at his soul.

Life at 18 can be hell for some…

It's a good thing he was mildly interrupted by what sounded like a car crash in his front yard. I say "good thing" in loose terms as he was subjected to a mild heart attack and a stream of images that would have sent any normal person into the psychiatrist. But these images helped him to write, they were the blood that moved the great machine of his creativity. In all likelihood I know that there really was nothing, a car had probably just started and backfired, but that doesn't mean that nothing *had happened*, or at least in this case…

Car crashes happen more in the mind than on the road…

Outside it was still snowing heavily and the snow was not melting off the yard as it so often did in Colorado. There looked to be quite a bit of it. But in the obscure fallings he wasn't sure how much of the forecasted four inches was there. I think that Johnny suspected that there was more than four inches. But I know that he planned on skipping the next day no matter the weather. The snow wasn't supposed to be that great, just in the same way a child isn't supposed to be buried by their parents.

But there's always things that aren't *supposed to happen*…

The irony that I spoke of in the beginning came in the form of a snow day, on a day Johnny was going to skip school, he didn't end up having to go to it. It's a good thing that there was a snow day. Knowing Johnny as I do, it would've ended badly for everyone had he stayed home alone.

It would've started with him using his stolen key to his father's liquor cabinet. He would drink himself to the point where he couldn't remember himself. Then he would slowly remember everything. It was there that he would lose it all. The anger would have taken him first, revenge, self-hatred, loathing… Those whose lives haven't been touched by the darkness don't seem to get these concepts when I talk to them, they wonder how some can hate life so much. If you've ever thought that, you got a lot to be thankful for, but I'll come out and say it; you don't have a clue. You don't understand some of the things I will tell you in this book no matter if you've seen a friend who's been like Johnny, you know Johnny, I don't give a damn if you have a PHD in psychology, unless you feel it, you don't have any sense of what it means.

Feelings are something that all other senses can't do. They seem to be a universally empathetic in my experience. They take a reality of one and translate it to another. If I, in telling this, don't make you feel what Johnny feels, then you don't know his story. But if I tell you his story, this story, and you know what it means to be him for just a moment, then I have done all that I can. I've told the story that he couldn't tell, the story that he entrusted to me so long ago, and to him that story means something.

I tell you; sometimes for Johnny the depression would seize him and never let him go. It was like straying into the woods, and then realizing he didn't know the way out, no matter where he turned the trees were always going to be there. People like to say that they know what it feels like to be hopeless; don't believe them until they have fought against depression. Because until they too have walked that path, they do not know it, they know *of it*, and that's a whole hell of a lot of a difference.

It's the difference of having walked the path and having looked at it…

It was always the anxiety that hit Johnny though not always the depression. Depression is like a giant boulder slowly crushing you. It's big and you're stuck underneath it and slowly it takes you on, squashing the life from you slowly, stealing the breath from your lungs. Anxiety on the other hand, that was a real nasty piece of work. It mugs you in a back ally and uses a rubber hose so that no one knows what happened. It hides among the everyday mundane things until all of a sudden like a precision ninja strike it would come out of nowhere to leave Johnny powerless. It came on to Johnny at the littlest things, and it too is just as dangerous as the boulder, except that it's shattered into a thousand pieces that are flying at you in all directions and you don't know where to turn, there's no escaping that either, no matter how good you are at dodging the rocks eventually they too will hit you. And not just one, because once one hits you, there comes another, and another, and all you want is out of the way but there is no turning back for anything. It just nails you as you sit there and take it. And you can only take so much…

But when it comes down to it, had it not snowed that night, Johnny would have killed himself…

But the thing is, it did snow.

Minor thing really, when it is placed under a 21ˢᵗ century lens. Unless there is a blizzard, it doesn't make the news, except during the 5 minutes of weather in the beginning. But I'm here to tell you it is the smallest things in the world that change it the most; we just don't know how to see it. We don't know how to see that by smiling to that kid in the hallway, he doesn't think that the world is too cold and decide to shoot up the school. We don't know how to see that throwing that little kid in the corner the football will start him down a path to NFL career. We don't know what we do in this world and it is always the littlest things that truly affect people. Driving a little slower, and all of a sudden you didn't get the speeding ticket. Saying goodbye to your grandparents, and all of a sudden *you got to say* goodbye…Taking a chance on the kid that no one else has, and suddenly you've saved their life because now it means something…if you don't take anything else from this book, then take this: *remember the littlest things in life change the biggest part of our lives.*

That night, in Elysium Colorado, you couldn't have seen your own damn feet when you looked down. It was a classic whiteout that just lasted for hours. I don't remember how many accidents there were from people too ignorant or too proud to stay off the roads. My guess is there weren't many, considering it would have been a miracle if you could find your car. So most people awoke that next morning to find that there was roughly a foot of thick wet snow covering everything; more in many places because the valley effect had lead to a large amount of gigantic drifts.

There was another part to the cold that morning. Johnny commonly had strange nightmares. Sometimes they were the garden variety of falling endlessly, other times they were strange, haunting ones. This night was one of the latter unfortunately. In his highly toned and creative mind, there was a level to the fear. When he talked about them there was one that struck me a lot more than the other ones that he had. In this one he was inside of Sara's room. It was just after the accident. There was a sense of the fear that dragged on him like a chain. Then suddenly the room would catch on fire and the flames would burn in bright red. All around him there was no escaping it. He could hear screaming from the accident. He could see everything spinning. Then suddenly there was nothing but shattered remains of a beautiful room. Everything was black and burnt and collapsing except for a door in the middle of the room made of wood that could not have been made by human hands. It was dark and twisted and the frame was not quite the perfect fit of the door that it held. In the small cracks underneath it a bright light came from the sides and illuminated the room hauntingly, making everything seem even more twisted. The air in the room is what he talked about the most. He talked about how the air seemed so heavy, how it never seemed to move, and that he felt like he was drowning in it…how you could see the dust particles just hanging in the air. And from the door came a voice not human, not of this earth…

"Johnny…"

He couldn't go towards the door though…he couldn't go to it…

Then he awoke to hearing his father yelling that he wasn't up yet…all a dream, he thought trying to shrug it off. He opened his window to see some fresh light. What he saw was snow as far as the eye could see.

It was a beautiful sight, Johnny thought, a place out of his story. A country called Delthamar, where a royal princess was from, where there was a beauty that never harmed anyone, a beauty that endured forever, unlike some things…. It had that simple elegance, that picturesque feel to it, something that some poor photographer sends into hallmark and it ends up on a Christmas card. A kind of beauty that endures forever and never seems real enough to be in that moment.

He didn't realize that there was a foot of snow covering everything in the town. He just flicked on the TV on the counter as he ate his cereal. There was a weatherman wearing a coat talking about how this huge winter storm had came through (everything was over exaggerated in the media as far as he was concerned). Power-outages, everywhere...Denver was a complete mess traffic wise...maps with what looked like 12 to 28 degree temps, except the weatherman was going nuts about various parts of them...and then there was something he didn't think that he heard quite right.

"That's right folks, 24 inches of snow in one night and more is still on the way!!"

How can that be, he thought, *there has to be a mistake*. But a look out the window confirmed it as the snow covered all the way to the window itself. Until that moment he hadn't really noticed. Then came the news,

"All schools are closed, that's right," The weatherman who Johnny highly suspected of being a pedophile, "All schools are closed. A snow day for all the boys and girls watching."

If that man can talk about kids and not get arrested, Johnny concluded, *there is something wrong with America.* But that was insignificant with the sudden joy in the pit of his stomach. He had the whole day to himself. There was no school, no facing the difficulties, he could just be alone for a little while, and enjoy himself for a few moments... Everything was different...

It was only perspective but that alone changes all...

I guess I can't really tell the tale of what happened to Johnny, without telling what happened to him before this whole day started. It's something that perhaps people remember, perhaps not. I tell it the best that I can with the story truth. Because that's what really matters.

It was about a couple months before, during the late spring, when he had taken his then girlfriend Sara out hiking in Denver. They had hiked several times; in fact they were celebrating their two year anniversary as a couple then. Everyone knows that kind of couple. They are inseparable, not because they are so in love, but because of something deeper. Like harmonic chords they seem to complete each other, strengthening the bond between each other. It was considered a sweet thing by most of the girls at Elysium high school. They were somewhat of a celebrity couple. Sara and Johnny went everywhere together and did everything with each other. Everyone thought they were inseparable.

Fate, unfortunately, thought otherwise...

After a long day of hiking, romance, love and passion, they were coming back through the mountains. As they passed through an intersection, they were T-boned on the passenger side, right where Sara was sitting, by a guy going almost 55 mph in a Ford F350 pickup. The sheer force of the impact alone was enough to send the driver of the F350 out of his car and it knocked Johnny's Jeep Ranger completely over coming to rest in a little spot by a small smooth flowing river known as Mystic Creek.

Those who saw the accident say that they will never forget it. The truck was smashed and parts of glass were everywhere. The smoke was billowing from Johnny's jeep that was turned upside down by the edge of the road by the corner of the river. The crowd of onlookers gasped as they beheld the scattered remains of a driver that had been ejected from the car was scrapped across the pavement like road kill. Out of the wreckage of the Jeep a kid pulled another body.

I wasn't there to see it firsthand but the screams that came from his mouth are said to have been inhuman. It was described by one lady as being like the howl of a feral animal, hauntingly echoing over the mountains and memories of those there. It was Johnny, or rather,

What was left of him…

In a scattered tangled mess of indecipherable scrap metal that had once been a Jeep, only one man emerged. Johnny once told me that the people in the crowd just stood there…horrified. He tried to move but his leg wouldn't budge. I remember him saying in one of his darkest hours that the walk to the car was walking into Hell. The way he described the nightmares were something horrifying, all the shattered glass, all the fire, all the pain, and the dread that only a man who knows what is in the car ahead of him could tell. I have to imagine that the walk back to the car would be like walking into the fires of Hell, into the mouth of the Beast, but Johnny knew that he had to do it. The pavement was hot and sticky with gasoline and melted tar as he pulled her from the wreckage. He said that he thought she was alive right until he looked into her eyes.

He said Mystic Creek reflected the majestic mountains in her eyes, not her soul. It put me to tears to hear it, and I can only imagine what Johnny saw…no trace of passion or love. There was just emptiness, the same feeling he now felt. Covered in his and her blood, he looked down for what seemed like forever, I'm sure. Hours ago those lips had been locked with his. Moments ago those eyes were looking with love, not staring blankly into the heavens unable to blink away the blood coming from her head...Only seconds ago, that head was thinking, and dreaming, not covered in blood. Not cold, not indifferent...

Not lifeless...

Sara had died that summer afternoon. There was no escaping it. Before that intersection, she was alive, and after that intersection she was dead. Cruel as it may seem, I think that what happened to her was better than what happened to Johnny. He was a very outgoing person junior year. By the end of summer, hardly anyone knew who he was...whether the person that had once been there was still left. And by the end of the first semester of senior year he was an untouchable. There was no one that crossed him in the hall, there was not one that said, "Come over to my party," or "let's go to the game on Friday," and that was one of the saddest things to see: when a man gets so sad that he drives away everyone around him. It was quite clear:

Two lay dead...three had died.

He wore a silver cross with her initials on it, under a heavy sweatshirt, even in late August when the air was dry and hot, as far as he was concerned, it could snow every single day. People didn't drive so fast when it was snowy, they took their time, and weren't always in such a God Damn hurry to get from one place to another...and as far as Johnny was concerned, the world was a cold place without Sara.

The only time people saw him was in class. He never talked. When he arrived at school, he would sit in the locker bay in front of her old locker, writing. The school at least did him the favor of not putting another person at it. Sometimes he wrote short stories, sometimes poems, sometimes a part to a novel, sometimes a part to a play, no one really knew. He dedicated them to Sara. They were really good pieces of work for a kid of his age too. I think that most of them could have been published if it wasn't for the fact that absolutely no one was allowed to read them. No one else would understand what was his rational.

Only one person would get to read his best works, and that person was Sara.

The teachers at his high school all knew about the accident. Everybody knows about something like that. Everybody knows, but nobody does. Everyone knows but nobody does anything different to try and help and try to change so nothing changes. Eventually the administration puckered up enough guts and ordered to go to the counselors, but that was a joke. I'm sure that it let a few administrators sleep soundly at the end of the night, and made sure that they felt a little better about themselves. But it did Johnny no good.

He sat there completely silent. It's one of the best ways I know to end a conversation. No matter what the question was he did not make any response. He might as well have been a statue for all the personality he displayed. You see the more he talked about her, the more he hurt. He was a shadow. A person people talked about. People knew what had happened to him, but not one of them understood or fully knew what he had been through. The accident was nowhere near the worst part...

Sleepless nights led to his insomniac nature. Pain led to more pain and more pain on top of that. He became a callous shell of emotional sensitivity. Think of it like a clam; hard on the outside and ooy-gooy on the inside. I know that sounds counter-intuitive, but the more he blocked it, the less he felt it, good or bad. The less he felt, the better things were for Johnny. It's best understood that when he was in pain that he couldn't do anything about it. It became so much that he lost his mind in the pain and the grief. He feared and hated that pain. It became to the point where he had to cut to keep himself alive.

When people learn that he was a cutter they think that he was looking for attention. Truth is when you are so deep in Hell that you have to cut, the rush of the pain... The sight of the blood...it feels good. For about thirty seconds Johnny was able to remember what it was to feel love...to simply *feel*...and the pain? Shit that was *normal*. So for him there was a thirty second escape that came at the price of his soul, the price of his dignity, the price of the few things that make a man a man. There was nothing left for him when he got to the edge, nothing left when he had to cut.

I guess it was the fact that he was really tired, or maybe it was the 4:00 AM bedtime, but whatever the reason, he decided to go to sleep for just a moment. And that's where the miracle that this day will become for him begins.

I have a tradition when I read stories: I read the last page first. Life is a journey, and all roads lead to the same place: death.

But it's how we get there that makes life so interesting.

So I will tell you the story. Johnny will end up at the end of today a different man than the one that I just told you about. See have I ruined the book? No. I have now made you curious as to the reasons how he ends up there, and that is where the true miracle of this tale resides, not in some cliché ending shown in every Disney movie.

Chapter Two
Janus

The following story, which I will tell, is something that needs to be explained before I can tell you what happened, else you would miss the point. Hopefully I'm not the first to tell you that there are things in life that do not make sense, life being one of them. The hardest things in life we cliché away so that we don't have to come up with an answer, or we simply admit that we don't know. It's a fundamental of human nature to believe that there are simple answers to complicated issues. This story is full of things that they tell you not to talk about, things they tell you not to feel things that they tell you are not appropriate.

Don't let them take this story from you…

Johnny was a depression case, he never received formal counseling on his grief, and he never took any Anti-depressants. There was a certain honor that he maintained that he was stronger for it, which I can honestly say that I am proud of him for it, even if it is the stupidest thing that he could do. Sometimes, I wonder whether this story has any meaning without that. I wonder whether there would be any meaning if he sat down and took a small pill at breakfast each morning to take away his grief, or whether there is something out there that can make people believe that there might be something that can make a man's heart change. People I know, that tell this story, don't tell it with the beautiful grotesqueries that make it the beautiful thing it is at the end they simply tell the truth and not the story…the truly beautifully grotesque story. That's right, a beautifully grotesque story…think of how water feels when you get a drink…now run 10 miles in 100 degree heat and tell me how that same water tastes. It's the perception that's changed and that is something that a prudent reader must keep in mind. Something in human nature makes us not like to see things the way that they really are, but rather see things for what they can be; this story is not like that, nor will it ever be. I will tell this story as best as I can to keep it accurate, and whether it is factually correct really doesn't matter. It's the truth that really matters and the truth of this story is what I have put down.

This is the saga of Theo Sandburg: He was a DI prospect middle linebacker, and had some serious power behind him. He was about 6'2" 260 lbs nearly all of which was honed muscle that accounted for his 81 solo tackles during the last season, a leader in the state, and nearly put him on the high school all American team. On the outside there was a respectable quality about him; an arrogant swagger, with matching good looks and a chest that could stop a bullet. On his letter jacket, he kept a skull and crossbones pin for every concussion that he had dealt out. Last time I checked there were 22 on there. He was the epitome of every bully cliché that I know of, yet every person in Elysium thought that this kid was the next best thing to Jesus Christ himself. Letter jacket, filled on sleeves, rock hard muscles, homecoming king, the pride and joy of the town of Elysium, and football captain and if you aren't getting skeptical of this kid by now, you should be.

Truth be told, he *was* all of those things, but those were a part he played. Shakespeare was right when he said, "all the world's a stage, and all the people merely actors." He was far different a person than the Theo Sandburg you read about in the headlines or hear the freshmen say that they want to be like.

In reality, he was a son to an abusive father, and a negligently indifferent mother, not much unlike Johnny. He was good at football because he knew that if his dad saw him miss a tackle, he would get his ass whooped raw via a coldly remorseless strip of leather that once held up his pants. He put the charm face on so that he didn't have to show society that he never really felt love. He made a smile on his face as he walked the halls knowing that there was no reason other than for the flesh on his bones that people even put up with him. For all that he said about Johnny being pathetic, he was worse as far as I'm concerned.

Theo was also a sociopath. For those of us without a psychology degree-*horribly* obsessed with violence and without a sense of remorse or wrong-doing. Since his freshman year, no person knew this better than Johnny did. When Johnny showed up to the nurse the first day of school after busting his lip open, no one suspected that a person like Theo could have thrown the medicine ball that hit him, nearly knocking out all of Johnny's bottom teeth. No one suspected that the bruise on his forehead was actually from a locker that he was thrown into, not that he "fell" into. Who would believe that the puncture wound in Johnny's side was from being shanked by a mechanical pencil?

I could go on for pages with the same basic things. There's an interesting trend to things though, something that people of Elysium, Colorado never realize; there's an excuse for everything. I will never tell you something that is sugarcoated, watered down, or in any way spun to fit my truth, but only to fit the truth.

The fact remains, because no one knew about it, because no one chose to care about it, so Theo continued to treat Johnny like a punching bag. I know, you think that there is a part where Johnny trains real hard to music that plays in the Rocky films, and then all of a sudden, he's big and buff and beats the shit out of Theo. It won't happen, don't think that it will happen; it's just the way things are. Johnny will never, and can never out physical Theo Sandburg. It's the way things are. Some people just don't want to accept reality.

The one thing that I can tell you that Johnny had on Theo was his mind. Inside that brain, Johnny could come up with some of the sickest, most sadistic and most painful ways to inflict pain on people. That's one of the things that people don't understand about Depression. People think that people who cut are ones that either want attention, or want to kill themselves. In reality, or at least Johnny's case, he wanted to put a real tangible reason to his pains and after he cut it was a rush of warmth that made him feel like he was loved again.

It's like when you get a brain-freeze from eating ice cream too quick. That pain isn't real, yet the only thing that you can do is hold your head.

That's the way it was for Johnny. He ached from a pain that wouldn't go away, and one that never really goes away. Sometimes, by hurting yourself you realize that one pain can silence another. I'm not saying if you stub your toe, stab yourself in the shin. I'm saying that for some, the only way that they can escape the pain is to make themselves hurt worse…Unfortunately Johnny knew that reality all too well. Though I hated to have seen him have to go through it the way that he was forced too, he came out the other end knowing a lot more than when he went in…

Chapter Three
Where It All Began

Johnny decided to go to bed after eating a breakfast at 6:30 so he could make it to school, only to find himself snowed in with more falling. He fell asleep by the fireplace. As he passed into his dream-state, he found that he was in the mountains once again, at a beautiful crossroads of a stream. It was a smooth stream, where the water moved in a silent current, barely making any sound except for the small rapids on the various rocks. It was peaceful serene and had a sense of holiness to it. It was as though there were forces at work there that were not seen normally on Earth. There was a surprising amount of color to the bright sunny woods, like it was all being amplified by a bright day. Johnny didn't like it to say the least. The fact is, something that should've felt good caused him a whole lot of pain.

He sat down on the log, feeling oddly conscious about the fact that in his dream he was able to see and to think. I guess that's the way it was for him during those dreams. I like to think that he was talking to some part of his consciousness, but I am no expert. Maybe Freud would know. But perhaps a cigar is just a cigar sometimes.

"Hey Johnny," Came a voice as he felt the log move from another person sitting down. He could even more oddly feel the water splash against him. It felt soothing and peacefully cold. Like a refreshing dip into a city pool on a hot day.

His heart, however, jumped when he saw who was looking at him…who he was sitting with. It was Sara.

"I felt that." She said pointing to his heart, "You need to calm down. I ain't gonna hurt you." Her voice was somehow different. It was as though she too was all part of this crazed sub-reality where the real was not real. All I know is it had to have been like a shot-put to the head to have seen his dead girlfriend back in full swing and seemingly unaware that she was dead.

"No…You're dead…" He said. In the past he had dreams where he thought she was alive again. But those hurt worse than the truth. Because in the end he went from feeling on top of the world to feeling the strain that Atlas must have felt.

"Am I?" She said lightly, "I can think of worse things. At least you remember me. Then I'm not really dead. If I live on in others memory, I have achieved a life after death, at least in the most primitive sense of the meaning." In the lightness of her conjecture there seemed to be something odd with Sara saying these things. It was as though dying made her some sort of an Einstein.

"I'm not getting you Sara." He said…the name even seemed to hurt to say.

"No, I figured that you wouldn't. Just try to comprehend what Vonnegut meant when he said 'If I exist in a moment, than I am always alive in that moment, no matter what happens otherwise'. It's a lot to try and comprehend I know, but try to do so." She said spinning her big toe in the lapping stream staring up at the mountains.

"You know I couldn't stand that guy…" Johnny began, and then tried to comprehend exactly what it meant, "OK. So why am I here? Why did you have to die? Why do I have to feel pain?" Johnny blurted out praying that maybe her new found intelligence would extend to questions that he was dying to have answered.

"Why you? Why anybody?" She snapped back with a retort smiling all the while, "I'm sorry Johnny, but there are always going to be questions. Sometimes you just have to realize that they don't always need an answer, as much as we would like them to have one. I can't help you with the deep philosophical questions of the universe. Someone else is probably better at explaining it." She said turning away and looking around smiling as though the answer lay in the beautiful scenery around them.

"You mean there are answers." Johnny said pressing the question.

"Only for those who can understand them." She said with a wink, "You'll understand someday. Put it from your mind for now." She said with a sense of finality as she rested her hand on his knee. It felt so real that Johnny could feel the goose bumps.

"OK, so are you in…" He couldn't bring himself to say it.

"Heaven?…no if I remember correctly this is Mystic Creek about 15 minutes drive from the accident. I had forgotten how beautiful it was…" She said in awe of the trees and the creek and the smoothness of it all, but then came back down, "As for the other meaning, right now, I'm in your dreams. In a couple minutes I'll be in my mother's prayers. Tomorrow, I'll be in yours and Stephanie's thoughts, and then the list goes on and on." She said lightly. To her it was almost like a pleasant chat over tea.

"Does your mother no good, if there isn't a Heaven." Johnny said bitterly and under his breath not realizing that Sara could full well hear it.

"I have neither affirmed nor denounced that there is or isn't a Heaven. It's not in my power to do so. But you never believed in a Heaven. So why do you give a rip?" She said with sorry eyes starring into Johnny's soul. His heart ached, but it was his pride that responded.

"I believe in something." Johnny said defensively.

"Really? That's a change from the Johnny I have seen lately." She said in a slightly challenging tone with an almost competitive smile that Johnny loved so much back when she was alive.

"I think that if, when a man dies, he is truly sorry for any wrongs that he has done, then he gets to live out eternity in the best moments of his life. I don't really think that there can be a place that is the house of God, if He even exists." Johnny said trying to read her responses all the while. He had struggled with religion ever since she died, and it had not gotten any better.

"The Lord works in subtly mysterious ways, my mother always said that…but you and her never got along that well… Anyway sometimes we don't realize why things happen until years after they happen. We may never know why things happen, but they happen and therefore have reason." She said shrugging her shoulders.

"OK, then what is the reason why you're here in my dreams. It seems like every time something good happens I am painfully reminded of you and I start the cycle all over again. I just want you back or to let you finally go, and one is impossible and the other is too hard to face." Johnny whined, his frustration getting the better of him.

Sara's voice wasn't controlled, it was soft and peaceful, "You have to realize at some point, my love, that it shouldn't hurt. I remember the words I last said to you, and as cruel as irony can be, they were true. The truest meaning of those words can mean nothing if they do the exact opposite to you than what they were intended to." She said with a deepness of the oceans.

"Why…that's all I want to know." Johnny said trying to remain calm.

"I told you, why me? Why anybody? Bad things happen Johnny, and the only true tragedy of this world, is that people aren't supposed to realize that they do." She said shrugging…placing her hand on his knee.

Then, quite suddenly, she slid off the log, and into the water. Her head barely bobbling above. Johnny quickly sent his hand down to help her up. But she would have none of it. There was a simple brilliance to seeing her there, yet Johnny wanted so badly to get her back.

"That's where you go wrong Johnny." She said with a smile, treading water in front of him as he grasped for something quite out of his reach, "You think that everyone else is in trouble. Sometimes, even though you look like you're up shit-creek without a paddle, it's not always a bad place to be." She said moving away from the log.

"Will I remember you when I wake up?"

"Yeah. But you probably won't remember this, at least not for a while. I just hope that maybe today you'll realize that the best part of life is the fact that you don't know what happens. We will all face death, Johnny. The only difference is that some hold their head high, and some have to be dragged into the arena…" She said, as she started flowing down stream, smoothly and peacefully.

"Wait!" Johnny yelled.

"I can't anymore Johnny. The water calls." She said and then suddenly Johnny found himself in his room, sweating and breathing heavily. He got up and got a drink. Somehow the thought of water made him feel more whole. He didn't remember the dream. But he did learn something.

He would think that conversation out, if not verbatim, close. He could hear Sara's voice inside his head. Whether he liked it or not, he could hear it. Think of it as a mild schizophrenia. I'm here to tell you that Johnny knew that wouldn't be the last that he would be hearing of Sara.

It's one of the hard things about loosing someone at a young age. Well, perhaps a young age, or maybe it's in the horribly violent way that they are taken, or perhaps it is all about the possibility that leads to thought of what may-be and what did happen I'm no expert and don't claim to have any clue as to how PTSD affects the average human psyche, but I do know how it worked for Johnny. In Johnny's mind there was a blender that took every emotion and memory and spun it for about three months. So what he had to look at now, was just a smeared mess of what had once been there.

So in his mind he was unable to tell what really took place, and what he knew took place. I can't tell you that he thought it took place. The mind is a very fragile thing at this age. To him, what he thought happened, he had dreamed about and remembered. I'm not saying that by thinking that she didn't die, that she didn't. I'm talking about him and her going out to a movie, even though they never saw it.

It's the pains like that that show the scars of an emotional tear. Things get so meshed up that a guy like Johnny ends up crying his eyes out every night, mainly in tearless sobs, and soundless screams, all over something that *may have* happened. A guy like him ends up with nights like this all the time. Something so wonderful, so great, so beautiful, touching him. But because he is so scared, the good feels bad. Whether you can comprehend this or not relies on your own experiences.

All of those pains though, that's what Johnny felt on a daily basis. It's a sad life. But as Sara said, "Shit happens."

Guess we all have to deal with it.

Chapter Four
The Snow Keeps Falling

When Johnny got downstairs, he knew that he had to shovel. It was something that he always did, and he didn't really mind that much. He put on a sweatshirt and a pair of gloves and went out. No fancy music player, no big bulky coat to keep him warm, just a pair of gloves and a sweatshirt. There were flurries still flying outside, but there were only reports that this snowfall was going to amount to five inches. Insignificant on top of a foot, but when you are lifting it all with a shovel, it still feels like a lot.

Johnny looked at the bare metal shovel, and the long driveway. He didn't know where to begin. There was all so much, as always there were so many places to begin. The problem was choice. That's always what the problem is. So many directions, so many different paths, but only one destination to which he wanted to go. That was the hardest part: deciding which path to go. And so he stayed in one spot, never moving, never changing, and forever trapped by the choice of the moment.

That's the way things were in his life. He knew so many ways of making things better, he just didn't have the courage to start, if my memory serves me correctly it's because he thought that everything he started would inevitably fail. He just didn't know where to begin...

The metal scraping the driveway was something that sickened him. He had hated that sound, but it was unlike the sound that haunted his dreams. That was metal striking metal, metal scraping asphalt, the horrible dry scraping, the way it makes people's ears cringe when they hear it. It's a horrible unholy sound that still haunts him to that day. Hearing it brought back memories; as much as he tried he couldn't really block everything out.

He looked up at the sound of a loud engine. The Millers were plowing their driveway. They were "nice" people; smiling faces without brains nor answers to any questions that Johnny really wanted answered. He had liked them once, but that was before the accident, that was before the mess. Johnny remembered how his dad and Mr. Miller would talk about race cars.

"Now me, I love Sprint Car racing. You ever seen them? No, hadn't thought so...you see they're really light cars that go around a dirt track and when these things wreck *they wreck*." He said a smile coming on to his face, Johnny seemed to think it was funny remembering how ignorant some people could be, or possibly how tactless they could be...

"What do you mean wreck?" His dad asked curiously, "I mean obviously when you have cars going at 120 miles an hour plus it's spectacular, but what's so different about these wrecks..." His dad asked without a clue that Johnny could hear, not that Johnny wanted to.

"They can go 20-25 feet into the air flipping 15 times, and you should see the mess they leave...I mean it's not really the greatest thing that the sport should be known for but that is something that people come to witness, how many days do you get to see that?" Mr. Miller said enthusiastically like any under-indulged adrenaline junkie. Johnny on the other hand felt like punching the guy.

One time is too many times, Johnny thought. I have to admit that he knew more about the wrecks than to think that a person only goes through the wreck once...They might only break their arm once from that wreck, they unfortunately have to go through it plenty of times at night, waking up in the cold sweats and the silent screams...he knew more about those wrecks than how many fans thought it was cool.

"It was rather unfortunate, the last race that I was at...they ended up taking the guy away with third degree burns. If I remember right, his gas tank caught fire...and the idiot just sat there burning up..."

Johnny just shook his head. Sometimes, I have to say that a man can only hear so much. Sure it's easy to sit there in the stands and ask why a guy didn't get out right away. There isn't anything up there that is as frightening as going through the wreck. Johnny remembered how hard it was to get out, not because of the fact that his leg was broken, but because of the shock. Johnny figured the guy didn't even know that he was on fire...poor bastard.

Then there was Mr. Miller's son, Carl. He was a young kid, about ten...maybe nine or so, and the kid just did not know how to shut up. I mean he would sit there carrying the entire conversation no matter what. I guess that comes with the age, but Johnny was none too caring about that. In some regards he wasn't sure how to judge how someone should act at any age. There was also the fact that he was absolutely obsessed with the X-men.

"Did you know that Wolverine is over 150 years old?" He asked sounded amazed even though he had referenced it five times that night alone.

"Yeah, I had heard something like that." Johnny said dismissively trying to get back to his writing.

"How about the fact that Colossus has skin that can't be broken, and if someone like Rogue touches it, that mutant power is transferred over."

"I think they've done that a few times." Johnny said thinking of what he would do with that particular power and a *particular* person to play Rogue...

"Who would you be, if you could be an X-man?" Carl asked as many kids ask the same crazy question of what someone was supposed to be in a choice between two things they will never be.

"I don't know." Johnny lied trying to get away from the subject. I think personally the only gift he wanted was time travel, or the ability to see the future, or maybe to bring the dead back to life. There were plenty of options of "powers" Johnny wanted. Most of them were things you wouldn't find on the comic book pages.

Powers such as knowledge of how to express what he felt about things. Powers like making others respect him. Powers such as the ability to make himself heal when he felt pain on the inside. Powers sometimes, aren't all that you'd want them to be, there all that you need them to be.

"Sure you do, you just don't want to tell me." Carl said, Johnny laughed now. Little kids are always the best lie detectors on emotions.

"Actually, I've always wanted to be like Nightcrawler." He said with a faint smile as he looked at Carl.

"Nightcrawler? All he can do is disappear and reappear?" He said as if to say, that's it? No more? There's nothing special he can do?

"Sometimes all a guy wants to do is disappear..." He said vaguely.

"I'd want to be Wolverine!" Carl exclaimed, "Healing powers! Nothing can hurt you! You can't die, you can sit there and get shot, have people rip you to pieces and then poof! You're back to normal! Wouldn't that be sweet if you couldn't die?" Johnny thought he felt a tear coming, "and then the claws!" And from there in he went into another half hour of talking randomly about nonsense and the comic world. Johnny didn't really pay attention after that.

For Johnny, it's hard enough to live in the real world, not to mention a fake world....I guess that's not entirely fair to say. In dreams he could will people back to life, give them all the personalities of a person they were when you remembered them best. He could make Sara live again in his dreams, a practice that he was trying to not do anymore. Although it felt good for the moment it tore him up on the inside so bad that he knew he wouldn't be able to take much more of it.

That's one of the reasons Johnny was so complicated. He didn't know where reality ended and where his mind took over. Every person who is reading this has made up some story to impress someone, or to relate to something I know you have, so don't lie. It's not a bad thing; it's just what he needed to do. Johnny did it to keep Sara alive. I think that's about the noblest thing that a guy can do. Trying to save a life.

When she died, he just would dream up a new life for her. She was buried, but they had gone to movies, gone to the Rockies games, he had kissed her at a school dance. He never knew what was real anymore and what was stuff that he just thought up. I imagine that Johnny remembered a time where Sara talked about comics, about being Wonder Woman, or Jean Grey. In reality she probably never picked up a comic book, but Johnny doesn't realize that here. He feels the connection to her, and to her death.

He shoveled and shoveled as much as he could. He felt the wind against his face and it felt warm for 30 degrees, it almost felt warm, sunny and there was fresh pine…he could see water running where he lifted the shovel. He could see water *there* too.

The day that they had been together for the last time, they had sat on a big thick log that ran across the edges of the stream that was mystic creek. They had gotten their feet wet that day too. They had talked about dreams of going to the pacific, or skydiving or becoming a doctor and a lawyer and a writer. All of that came rushing back as his sock got thick and heavy with the water.

He shoveled and he hit his side. His keys to the car fell out and of course he didn't realize it till about a minute later as the snow kept falling. There was a feeling of panic. He searched around and he couldn't find them. He pulled them out and realized that unlike some things they weren't ruined…The anxiety was something that I can tell you he was "used to"…truth be told there isn't a man alive that can ever get used to the sudden blood flow to the brain…the sudden paralyzing feeling in his chest…there is something about that that makes it worse every time that he got it.

About five houses down the street were the Smiths. They had two little kids that were maybe ten years old each. They had built a snow man. A man that could be broken, but then rebuilt the same as he was before…and Mrs. Smith was outside in a bright red hat, and she was taking pictures of the two kids having fun.

He had taken pictures as well…

A small disposable camera that he had taken with him, Johnny remembered. It was a piece of junk that didn't really work right. He had taken it with him up that day, and he and Sara had plenty of pictures up by Mystic Creek and Blackstone Ridge. *I never found that camera in the wreckage*, he thought, not that he went looking for it. He assumed that it had burnt up along with the remains of his Ranger.

By now he had cleared a small pathway. He wasn't sure where he was going, not that he ever was. There was a certain feeling to trying to shovel the snow. He knew where he had to end up, but he didn't know how to get there. He knew where he had to be in life too, but getting there was a problem too.

Sometimes, we all have snow drifts in our path...

As he started to get tired, he noticed that across the way, the Millers were completely done. They had a big snow blower they attached to their John-Deer Riding Lawn Mower.

Some people get all the luck...

I would be a liar if I didn't tell you that I had seen him look up when he got tired. I have to imagine that he thought that Sara was looking down at him. Therein lies the problem for Johnny. That moment was absolutely beautiful. The snow stopped for a moment, and the clouds were thin enough to shine down on Elysium. The way that the light shined of the snow made the world stand still. It's a sight that would make every man feel free.

Having spent most the morning shoveling snow, he decided he would see what the rest of the town was up to. The roads were getting better, but he decided to walk, or more likely traverse the hills that had been caused by the snow plows.

Chapter Five
The Mask of a Shell

One of my favorite parts of telling the story of this day is what exactly happens to Johnny is very different than most people expected. But Johnny was a master in the art of outward deception. You'd figure him to stay locked up inside all day, but Johnny knew that there was more to life than just his pain. Most people that are deep in depression are that way. He fought like a champ or believe me he'd have committed suicide long ago. Unfortunately on some level he knew that he was going to escape his shell, and that he almost enjoyed living as the Johnny that other people sometimes saw. It was like acting out a character in his plays...

Except the stage was everywhere here...

Now I haven't looked up snowball fights in a dictionary but I'm guessing it would reference a small group of people just running and throwing them at each other not exactly planned; no armaments, no strategy, no weapons. Snowball wars on the other hand are quite different. Elysium was a place where things like this could happen. Maybe it was the small community setting, maybe it was the fact that there was a bunch of kids that started the tradition years ago. But to an outsider the thing seems absurd. I mean how many people actually create different forms of artillery for a snow ball fight? In Elysium, there was such madness and they knew how to create

First, Johnny's favorite: a snow canon. It is based on a potato gun made out of PVC pipe and a compressed air canister that screwed in the back. Turn the canister door and all of a sudden there is a rush of 50 psi that propels the snowball out with enough power to shatter plywood provided that the snow is hard enough. The best part is that you can put anything you want in them so there is some serious damage that can be done. The high schoolers bring about 15-20 of these canisters on each side, and then there are the inflatable intertubes that work as personal shields deflecting all but the most punishing blows, a nice asset when all you are fighting off is snow... They also build up plywood reinforced walls covered in snow to create a mini war environment. Because sometimes playing the game is a lot easier than the real thing.

Then there is the set up. One side takes the hill surrounding the jungle gym fort, the other the jungle gym. Usually it ends with stalemate, with wave after wave crashing into the fort until it finally ends or they give in. The tales of dramatic turns were usually the content that was argued at Al's Cheeseburgers during the winter months. Johnny felt so detached from it all. He watched as everyone talked about it, argued about it, and in the end he resented them for it. I guess it was more on the fact that they could care about such trivial things. They could care so much about things that never really mattered. They could care so much, and he couldn't care any less. He resented the laughter, he felt the pain, yet they said a snowball hurt. He wanted so badly to reach out and grab them. He wanted them to feel as he did. He wanted them to hurt like him-to fell like him-to hurt-to explode-to just have to be like him.

"Hey Johnny! He heard as he was passing towards the playground. Snowballs were flying, kids were hiding behind little barricades hand built while hiding.

Johnny ran through the snow to join the upper classmen that were standing there. It was Tony Jones, a burly and excitable senior, who had barricaded himself behind a wall of snow that was slowly crumbling.

Tony had known Johnny only since the accident. I would assume that he knew of Johnny before the accident. In all fairness to him he befriended Johnny, but never on the same scale as Johnny and Sara had been. Tony saw Johnny on levels that I'm sure Johnny never could understand. He had lost his dad at the age of thirteen. But Johnny couldn't deal with the loss as Tony could. Johnny never really was open with him. I mean sure he talked but Tony only got to the edge of the cliff, and he never looked over the side.

"What's happening Tony? What's the situation we got?" Johnny asked putting on the mask that he was so accustomed to wearing. Putting on the fake smile, the look of outward solidarity, the defense that he had against the emotional equivalent of artillery fire.

"Same old shit...the freshies are barricading themselves in the tunnels and they've got some artillery now so we can't seem to get near them." He said and as he did there was a scream as a girl got nailed by one of the heavy artillery shells.

"Damn it, that was Stephanie...Give me one of those launchers." He said with a vengeance in his eyes. Tony was not known as a very merciful person. He was known as having quite a good shot with a snowball.

Tony gave him a long thick pipe and Johnny compacted a snowball hard enough to withstand the force of going through the pipe. He then put it in the end and screwed the pipe shut with the compressed canister. He put it on his shoulder looking to aim for someone.

"Where's my freshie..." He muttered as he looked slowly.

Then he saw the kid who had shot Stephanie before. He took aim as the kid was running toward the tunnel. He then turned the compartment separator from the barrel to the compression chamber. A rush of air and a loud "Bumph" came out of the end of the tube with a small smoking end.

The kid was hit square in the chest propelling him off the tower and into a slide where he rolled all the way down apparently unharmed as there was no scream from broken bones and the ground was too soft from the snow to knock him out cold. That was not to say that it didn't hurt, but there was no permanent damage.

"Nice shot!" Tony exclaimed slapping him on the back.

I think that for a fleeting moment that Johnny was smiling. He might have actually felt free; I think that I remember him letting out a smile. Like the ice and snow below him, his mask was cracking slowly and surely.

For nearly ten minutes, wave after wave crashed at the underclassmen fortress like waves on the beach. Each time they went, there was little to no affect. Like the waves the crashed and then receded, still the sand was always there. Slowly they chipped away leaving less resources and a growing sense of desperation. Something that Johnny was used to. So in the worst times for most, he was right at home, he even might have been looked at like a leader.

"OK I got a plan, you remember how to pull a two-for-one charge?" Johnny asked feeling that there was something that needed to be done if they were going to win.

"Is that the crazy plan where I plunge head first at them holding something as a shield, and you and someone else shoot? Yeah, that's suicide now. These canons *hurt*, Johnny." He said dodging the large snowball thrown at him.

"Yeah, but we're going to be the distraction running straight at them from the back of the slide. Take that saucer there. We'll serve as a distraction and then we'll have a large scale charge on the lines."

"You're crazy…" Tony said shaking his head.

"I'm moving up, this morning I was just an asshole." Johnny joked, "How many canisters we got left?"

"Bout ten left." Tony said looking in the crate that they had brought them in.

"I'll reload to have one clear shot at their sophomore generals. Spread the word to everyone and hand out these canisters. One good firing should take them out."

He was right, there he was he ran as fast as he could right behind Tony, and for lack of a better term the plan worked.

Things work out…sometimes…

But one of the things I love to point out to people is something that people don't tend to see when they remember this day. Johnny wasn't sitting in the corner at all times, but that doesn't mean that he ever left it. Everyone I know has a split personality…

Johnny was no different.

To Tony, Johnny was a survivor. He was a bit *different*. He saw Johnny's obsessive writing as his way to cope with the horror he had experienced. After all, having seen something like that, anyone would need a way to cope with it. He too had felt for Sara, he was just as shocked. He had cried hard at her funeral, but for him it was something that had happened and now was over. That wasn't true for Johnny. Yeah, he saw the tears in Johnny's eyes when Sara's name was mentioned. I don't deny that he wanted to talk with him, but he didn't know what to say. But just to hear words, even if they seemed to be in an alien language, they would help more than silence could ever help.

But as with so many things like Johnny had experienced, it never happened. There was no denying that Johnny had gone so far as to believe that he had talked over it with Tony. He would have talked about how he felt. He would have talked about the darkness, and how it never seemed to go away.

And while he never said anything, and Tony never really figured out what happened, the fact of the matter was that Johnny was changed by the experiences that never happened. He was different around Tony, he might have even trusted him. I know it sounds odd. But around Tony, Johnny was about as close to free as he was going to be.

Chapter Six
Eruption

When the day ended, everyone was starting to get hungry and many were heading off to Al's Cheeseburgers, looking for a bit of soul-food and a place to eat. Johnny was invited with. It was a rare occasion to a guy like Johnny. He wanted it, yet he was afraid of it. For so long he had defined himself by the very chains that bound him to the darkness inside himself. For Johnny, seeing the bright spots in life lead to a pain. So Johnny kept to what he knew.

When Johnny left he wanted to go to the cemetery nearby and pay his respects to Sara. It was something that he had done for every single day since the funeral. I don't want to say that it became part of his routine because that would take away the sincerity of it. By making it a "part of his routine" it would seem as though it were an obligation to be fulfilled. He was walking across the frozen tundra when he was hit with something very blunt and cold in the back of his head.

"Who made you the fearless leader, you little prick?" Came an all too familiar voice, one that made the anger rise in his chest. A voice that made his eyes narrow and his fist clench tightly.

It was Theo Sandburg, and the cold object he realized was a snowball as he felt some of the shrapnel going down the back of his shirt. He felt no pain, the rage made sure of that. Over the years he had learned how to make himself nearly immune to pain when he was in the heat of a moment. Weather that was sliding a sharp piece of metal across his wrists or getting his ass whooped by Theo.

Now I know that there are people who are asking, how did he end up there, and it is just that-I don't know. He just did. And frankly that isn't something that needs to be debated, Theo showed up and they were all alone in the middle of the snow everyone else having gone off to Al's for Cheeseburgers and Chicken strips. They were all alone in the small field before the cemetery.

Mano-y-mano...

"What the hell, Theo? Can't you see I'm going to a cemetery? Can't you ever fuckin give me a second of peace?! What the hell is your problem?!" Johnny said screaming at him, his emotions getting the better of him. A costly mistake as the past had shown, but then again when had Johnny learned from the past?

"One word: you...that's my problem, but who asked you to talk, you piece of shit." He said as he backhanded him across the face.

Johnny felt his eyes tear up and blood started to run in his mouth. He turned around to a fist right in the face. The cold outside made the blow sting and Johnny knew that part of his nose was now lodged in his skull.

"You don't ever learn your lesson do you?" Theo said spitting on him as Johnny was on the ground wiping the blood on his sleeve.

Johnny made a quick move to his pocket where he pulled out a bottle and held it at Theo threateningly.

"This is Hypochlorite, and what's even better is that it is completely undiluted." He lied holding the bottle out, he then used angry sarcasm, "Now for today's science lesson. When I break this over your skin, it's going to hurt like hell as it starts bleaching away anything on your skin no matter how dilute it gets..., but what's even better is that I can throw it into your eyes...know what happens when you combine the two, do you?"

"No...but you aint gonna like what I do to you afterwards you little punk ass bitch." Theo said through clenched teeth.

"Hypochlorite is what they use in bleach and in this state, it's dangerous. So when I give you a shot of this to your face, not only will it eat through most of your skin, you'll loose your sight, which probably is a good thing, because you don't want to know what you're going to look like when it boils every part of your head. I'm no football expert, but

43

I know you have to see, and what will you be left with? Nothing. Exactly the same position I'm in."

"You're bluffing." He said smugly.

"Call me then." Johnny said menacingly.

There in lies his mistake. Because Theo took his foot and kicked Johnny in the crotch so hard that he very well could have broke his pelvis. And as Johnny fell forward, Theo wound his leg up again and kicked Johnny under the chin, knocking him out.

Now I didn't witness it first hand, but my guess is that Theo spat on him afterwards and kicked him a few times. He probably threw in a few cheap-shots, it wasn't unheard of on this case. Theo wasn't one to fight fair, and Johnny was the one that knew this very well.

I guess the volcanoes don't stop after the top blows off, an eruption continues...

Chapter Seven
Backseat Driving

Johnny found himself inexplicably in the back seat of his Jeep Ranger, and what was even worse is that he saw a younger version of himself driving and Sara was sitting in the front seat, but she was also sitting in the back next to him as well. It felt surreal, dream-like and there was a sense of almost what he could describe as being a movie. He felt different than he had felt in a long time. There was no logic about anything, but yet everything seemed to work with the same natural laws.

"Welcome back, Johnny." Came an all too familiar voice, one that he longed to hear again, but not like this. This was wrong, this was not the way that he was supposed to see her again.

"Sara!" He exclaimed, "you're…" He began almost hopefully, but then reality hit him like a shot-put to the head, "no…this is all a hallucination. I can't keep doing this to myself, I…can't….God…just…" He finished with his head in his chest trying to block it all out but it wouldn't go away.

He tightened every muscle in his body as though he was getting attacked. He was in pure defense mode but there is no defense to this. Every ounce of adrenaline was raging through him in a way that was almost impossible. He looked like he was about to be physically assaulted.

But you can't shield yourself from the future…

"Work with me here, I'm going to need your cooperation here if I'm to get anything out of this pain you are about to feel." She said putting her hand on his shoulder. A feeling that felt so real, yet couldn't be real.

"I can't work with you, Sara. This *isn't real...*" He said moving his arms around the back seat like a child throwing a temper tantrum.

"You know damn well as I do that this was real." She interjected coldly, "Yeah, we weren't sitting in the back of the Ranger, but you know, just like I do, where this ride ends." She said as they rode along on the way down towards the town. It was a cold and awkward silence for him.

I have to admit, that she seemed like a person watching a movie that they know how it ends. It sounds cruel, I know, I'm not justifying what happened, and personally I think that hurt Johnny worse than anything else did, the fact that she didn't feel like he did. Imagine sitting there knowing that the person next to you is going to die in a matter of minutes, and you can't do a damn thing about it. I can tell you it feels like your gut is hit with a sledge hammer. All of a sudden every ounce of energy is stripped from you, and nothing that you can do. You feel like purging everything from your system...like a toxic poison is spreading through you...

But there's nothing that you can do...

So what do you do when you know the future? You do what any man would do-try with every last breath to stop it from happening.

Johnny jumped out of his seat, and grabbed the handbrake that was sitting there and threw all of his weight behind it but it didn't budge an inch, the Jeep kept going down Blackstone Ridge following along a little stream that would be colored red with the blood of the two sitting in the front seat of that car. I have to imagine that the thought popped into his head whether that water was to be the same that washed their blood away as it peeled off the cement? Did the stream know that it was going to carry their blood in a matter of minutes? Did it know the blood it would soon be carrying? So Johnny screamed into his ear as loud as he could, "STOP!!! WAIT!!!GO BACK!!!" He pleaded tears starting to fall and he gave up and started to curl up into a fetal position, "Just kill me!" He sobbed, "What did I do to deserve this? God! Why!? JUST KILL ME!"

"Don't bother screaming to God, He ain't going to hear you, at least not *here* anyway, but I unfortunately can. So would you mind shutting up babe, cuz' I didn't come here to hear you screaming. I've heard that before." Sara said pulling him back by the back of his jeans.

She felt so real that a shiver went up his spine…

"OK, why are you here?" He said, wiping the tears off his face.

"I think that it's time you see things from my side of the accident. Now you remember where we were that day?"

"Blackstone Ridge. It was so beautiful, it was wonderful, we hiked all day…I wrote you a poem then…you and I kissed and made love for hours by that ridge, overlooking the world…how could I forget it…" He said holding back the tears the best he could. He was failing miserably.

"Yes, it was beautiful. You have the camera from that day. Or rather there was one, I know who has it now. You'll come across it soon. So the story as I remember is that we were talking about our futures, once we got out of high school that is. Do you remember that?" She asked loftily looking out the window at the brilliant scenery.

"You wanted to be a lawyer down in southern California, so you could visit the ocean; I wanted to be a doctor. I wanted to help people." Johnny said holding back tears.

"And you still do. Somewhere deep inside of you, lies the urge to help people on a scale that the world could use a little more of." She said smiling faintly while her eerie stare looked at him.

She looked and felt so real…Nothing had changed…

"I wish I could change this…" Johnny said, still looking terrified, "Do we have to do this here? Can we talk up by Mystic Creek?"

"Mystic Creek? You remember the name…but you don't remember the place. Not the way you should, Johnny. You don't remember how beautiful it was, you remember the water turning red with young blood. I remember the feel of it on our skin, how it flowed so pure…You remember it as the last place that it was alive…you remember the horror…" She said reminiscing, "I want you to see something." She said and suddenly the scenery blurred.

"I know why you can't sleep at night. Why you hurt when you talk, why you can't seem to breathe or relax. I think it has to do with this part, right here. I was a fool then." She said, her smile was fading.

"It's too damn cruel to make me witness it again, don't, Sara. I thought you loved me, why put me through this agony again?" He said hoping that this Sara could reason with him.

"If you go through this thinking that you will be in pain, then agony you will find. But I offer you something more, something that you have never considered, something called inner peace. You haven't felt that in years. Some part of me wonders if you even want to?" She said bitterly.

"How can I find peace when my heart is in pain, Sara?" Johnny said holding back some tears.

"Problem with pride is that when you loose your hand to the blade, you stick your arm out to get it. Now that doesn't sound that sane does it?" She asked rhetorically, then continued, "You must learn to let go of me. If I thought that it would be easy, do you think that I would be here? You and I both know this. The question here is whether you are going to fix it…" She said with a faint smile and a piercing look into his soul.

"How can I let go of you?"

"You were going to have to at some point. I had no intention of living forever nor did I want to. I don't think you realize how little time left I had."

"But you only lived sixteen years." Johnny protested. To him that was too young to die. Foolish phrase if I have ever heard one…too young to die…explain that to the mother who is informed that her little son did not survive the operation. Explain that to the father that just saw his son ride his bicycle out into the street only to find a pair of headlights waiting for him…

"But in those sixteen years I lived, Johnny. Something you would do well to remember. I lived more in that day with you, than many will live in a life time. A heart beating doesn't make you alive or dead, letting your soul experience the world, now that is living. Having an effect on people, changing those around you for better or for worse, now that is what life is. But you seem to hate living, even at your own absurd definition, and I must ask…why?" She asked sounding broken hearted.

"Because I feel guilt having lived and you died. I hate myself for not being in your position. You had offered to drive…it would have been me there. It should have been me there."

"I can't blame you, and no one should. You would be amazed at how many little decisions in our lives change their outcome. It would be unfair to blame you, or anyone, because in your position I would be doing the same thing. But I think babe that you need to learn that life can only be lived foreword, and understood backwards. Like I used to tell you Johnny-." She started.

But Johnny cut her off, "Why me, why anybody? But if I might ask-." And he too was cut off.

"The last thing that I ever said, when we reached that stop-sign, was '*I feel so good right now, I could die*'," and suddenly the car was frozen in time, then the Sara in back seat continued as though it were in virtual reality, "The only problem is I never got to tell you the last part, which was '*and be happy*'."

The car door started to smash in slow motion, Sara opened the door, and Johnny followed her out, "Roughly a tenth of a second later, I was dead. Blunt-force trauma to the skull completely destroyed my brain, but for what it's worth there wasn't much there to begin with." She said, making a joke about her own death, which Johnny found both utterly repulsive and humorously ironic at the same time.

"Why did it have to happen like this?" Johnny asked and started to get angry, "If I was only a second later...one..." He counted off dramatically, "and both of us would be alive."

"And one second earlier and you'd be in a small 7x4 box six feet under the earth just like my body is. Bet you never thought of that, did you?" She said with a laugh.

"I should be-." Johnny began his head digging back into his chest.

"You know what I would give just to be able to see you with my own eyes? I would sell my soul away for the rest of eternity, just so I could kiss you one more time. I would make a deal with *Satan himself* if it meant that I would see you again in the flesh and blood. For *that one second*...to everyone else in the world, it doesn't matter, but for me, I would sell my soul to get to change it again. Think of all the time we waste, and then what we wouldn't give to have the smallest fraction of it back...To step on that pedal as hard as I could or grab the wheel and make sure everyone got away, but I can't. I never will be able to nor will you. You however have a choice."

"To be or not to be, eh?" Johnny said reciting Shakespeare, "to live or die."

"No, to live or die is not your choice anymore. I've seen a lot of dead people with more life in them than you have now Johnny. You get the choice that I never had, to die, or to live again…." She said and then she walked away to the water, and waded in and she disappeared.

Chapter Eight
Melting the Ice

"Johnny? You OK?" Came a female voice somewhat high pitched, Johnny could hardly see who it was nor could he figure out where he was.

"Yeah...where...am...I?"

"The school. You were out cold..." The voice said sounding familiar but distant, almost like the echo Sara's voice was becoming in his head. It was slightly frightening but yet it carried with it a little less weight than her voice had.

His eyes regained focus and he got to his feet. He was in the high school, right by the pool, he could smell the chlorine and it felt really humid. In front of him was a smiling face of Stephanie Mathews, a girl he had known for quite a while, but as of late had not really seen.

She was taller than Sara, with lengthy dark brown hair and an air about her as though she was absolutely untouched by the darkness. It was like she had a smile that the darkness couldn't touch...an immunity to the world around her that Johnny just couldn't comprehend. It was hard for Johnny to see her. She had known Sara but she was so untouched by the loss. She seemed to always be smiling and when he looked at her popularity he almost loathed her....she was everything that he was not, everything that he was supposed to be, everything that might have been and a reminder of everything that he had failed. As he shivered she smiled and suddenly everything seemed warmer...

Smiles weren't something that he was used to seeing...

"What in the hell are we doing here?" He asked looking around and completely oblivious as to how he got there or how long he had been out. All he knew is that he had a nasty cut and that his genitals hurt quite badly.

"Well, I had a key and you have a nasty cut on your face, this was the easiest way to medical attention that I knew of. Come on, this way." She said laughing leading him down the hall to the girls locker room entrance opening the door opening it up.

"That's the girls' locker room. I can't go in there." He said dumbly.

"You really took one to the head, Johnny. We're the only ones here in the building, so what does it matter? Come on, I don't want that thing getting infected." She said pointing to Johnny's busted skull.

He put his hand up to his head that was hurting severely, and he felt the trickle of the blood, he saw it in his hand as well. He felt a shiver on his spine and a sudden rush of adrenaline.

He had seen enough blood for one lifetime...

"I saw your arms and neck, were those scars all from the accident?" She asked completely casually. Most people were very touchy about that sort of thing, she jumped in head first.

"Yeah, got over 100 stitches in all. It didn't even look like me when I got out of the hospital. Never really looked like the guy I once was..."

"Yeah you looked a lot better back then. Then again, you weren't moping around everywhere..." She jabbed.

"How did you get a key here?" Johnny asked preferring not to take on the insults.

Stephanie smiled, and looked at him fondly, much like a proud parent, "Sara gave me this about a month before the accident." She said.

She then looked away and smiled, fondly remembering times together. If it was an act it still had a great affect. Johnny felt deeply cut, a sort of shame, and a mixture of self-hate and sadness that always came with such things...

"Yeah, Sara...damn that was a shame...How have you been doing on that?" She asked lightly. It sounded sincere, but the way she asked it seemed so light hearted so fresh and easy, as though simply asking how are you...

"No offense or anything, but I don't like to talk about that..."

Sara laughed, I imagine Johnny would have felt a rush of anger, if not for how easily she was talking about it, for the jibe at him. He was beyond angry.

"Nah, what you really want to say is, '*why in the hell do you care Steph*'...well Sara was one of my best friends, and in her best interests, I think I need to keep track of you. Make sure the spirit that lived in her lives on in you." She said wrapping an ace bandage on his head stopping the bleeding, then muttering, "well it'll have to work."

"I forgot you and her were best friends...Everything kind of went though the blender...I haven't been able to think straight since the funeral."

"You were still in the hospital when that happened. But I understand when you say that you haven't thought straight...none of us have." She said patting him on the back, "here let's have a sit." She said affectionately.

"Where?" Said Johnny half confused half hurt with emotions running over the edge.

"Right here, legs in the water. Come on it's nice." She said and she pulled off her sweat pants to a pair of short Carolina blue shorts. Johnny rolled his jeans up and took off his shoes.

The water felt cool and refreshing...

"So how do you really feel?" Stephanie asked as if she could almost already tell that there was some part of him that was holding back. Johnny knew that she was only meaning the best but he couldn't seem to get over the fact that she was still so easy going about things that meant life and death to him.

"Fine..." Johnny said.

"No you don't, but I'm sure you'll get there someday. I guess it's different for all of us. I mean for me it was hard at first but then it got better. I know it will get there with you too..."

"Yeah, well you don't have to live everyday with that image in your head. I know that it's a tragedy but you weren't there to feel it..." Johnny said partially proud partially angry.

"I actually went down there. To where the accident was. Right by Mystic Creek, you know that place still amazes me. Sara used to talk about it all the time, said she loved how you would take her there. But my guess is that you haven't been there since the accident."

"Would you?" Johnny asked looking somewhat awestruck that she would even suggest such a thing.

"Yeah, I go every Sunday and put a rose by the water where the Jeep went in. I still can see the crash at that intersection whenever I look at it." She said and she paused.

But after pausing she revealed the fundamental difference between those like her and those like Johnny, "I also see the mountains across the creek. The way it flows is beautiful. There is a good reason that it is called mystic creek."

"I wish I would have left. Perhaps only a second earlier and she'd be alive."

"Or you both could've died?" Steph said, "We don't know. One thing I know is that when Sara went, she went happy; she went free and on angel's wings she soared on. She told me once that the mountains were God's gift to show that he does exist. Something as beautiful as anything can possibly be, yet as bold and mighty as they need be. I envision her seeing those as the last image she ever saw, or perhaps you…I think she'd have liked that as well." Stephanie said with a small smile.

"Did she talk much about me?" Johnny asked, "I never got to ask her." There were so many things that he never got to ask her. So many things that he would have liked to have asked her but that was too late now…he had to get over that if he was going to be getting any answers to the questions that most deeply troubled him.

"All the time, Johnny. All the time…she used to say something that I only recently got to see."

"What's that?"

"She said that you had the spirit in you." She said looking at him smiling in a way that seemed to make the water warmer, and the room brighter, "She always used to talk of a spirit inside you that was so wonderful, something like a mystery of a person. She used to say…oh what was it…*you had the spirit in you.*" She said pointedly.

"Really?"

"Johnny, you know she didn't die so that you could be in pain. There's enough of that going around. You don't remember that week before she died do you?" She asked suddenly at the end as though there was a small revelation.

"No not really." Johnny said truthfully. He had focused so much on the day itself that he really didn't remember what had happened that week at all.

"I remember it. She was diagnosed with lung cancer. She knew she was going to die, when I don't think any of us will ever have known. But there was a bit of a miracle in her death in that car accident; she never suffered." Stephanie said splashing a little water with her foot.

"No...she didn't...she wouldn't...she would've told me..." Johnny said crying hard as it hit him.

"She told me not to tell you. I think she just wanted to go peacefully and I think that is about the most peaceful way she could have gone."

"What?"

"Think about it, she didn't suffer like she would have with the cancer. She just *went*, and it was quick and easy, no pain, nothing harsh, nothing painful, *she just went*. Everyone around here has this horrible connotation about how if you die a violent death that it is somehow horrid. One moment she was alive, the next she was dead, and all the suffering would have been gone. And now she's up in heaven waiting to join us."

Now I have to imagine that it was at this point in the conversation that the ideas started to click for Johnny. Now don't get me wrong, Johnny had sat there and thought about it for a while, but he never knew about the cancer, he never knew about how she would have died anyway. His biggest pain was the fact that he lost her and he didn't even know that she was going to go.

Now all of a sudden there is a tide shift, herein lies the Act IV revelation where by the plot twist is expressed and everyone starts to figure things out, if you're looking for the cliché. Now I'd be a liar if I told you anything other than what I know, but I will give you the story truth, Johnny was breaking out in tears by the end.

Whether or not his tears actually flowed down his face is known only by Johnny and Stephanie, the only two people that were there, and I don't think that either of them really cared so much as to say one way or the other.

Sometimes I have to admit that Sara was right, there is actually purpose in this world, 'cuz why Johnny? Why now? Sometimes you don't need to know the answer, you just have to accept that it is there. The accepting of the fact that things are out of our control is the hardest thing in human nature, but it is one of the most real, one of the most powerful things when we finally came to terms with it.

I don't wanna make it sound like Johnny flipped on a switch and everything was alright. Like the darkness just suddenly left. It was not that way at all. But in looking back on that day, he told me that is when it all changed for him. Everything started making sense, but his day was far from over.

And others would be looking back on this day as the day everything changed...

Chapter Nine
Karma

While Johnny was getting attended to by Stephanie Mathews another, lesser known event of that day happened. I say lesser because no one really cared about this kid after the fact. When sports fans in Elysium looked back I guess they would say that this is where it all went wrong. Now when Theo beat the living shit out of Johnny he had a purpose, just like everything in life there was a reason to it. There are few that knew that Theo Sandburg actually loved Sara.

That's right the same Sara that got killed in the car that Johnny survived in.

Now Theo loved to express his emotions, and what I mean by that is pound the piss out of anything that angered him. He never told Johnny why he beat the crap out of him, he just did it. Actions speak louder than words was the motto he lived by.

When he beat Johnny to a pulp he continued on into the wooded cemetery, and walked to Sara's grave. He knew the way whether it was covered in snow or not. It was on top of the hill about a quarter mile's walk and it was a large tall rectangular headstone mounted on a marble base by a tree. It was saddening to look at, but yet there was something to it that made it feel a little bit serene. Perhaps it was the way the light reflected off the snow; perhaps it was the smell of pine in the air. I don't honestly know, but I do know that something sparked a hatred in Theo's heart.

The same way that beauty created depression in Johnny, the beauty created anger in Theo. It's what allowed Johnny to write for so many years and what made Theo such a dominating presence on the field. Funny thing perception…I guess that's just the way that things were.

"You had to go with him." He said violently, and he spat the blood out of his mouth and it landed above her headstone, "If you would've dated me then you would be alive and he would be the one that lies here." He shook his head again, "I loved you Sara, but you chose this. I don't know why you ever meant anything to me, you had to go and get yourself killed with that stupid son of a bitch Johnny, and now look. Well I guess that's Karma for you isn't it?" He said and he turned away.

As he walked away he slipped on the snow and his leg twisted violently as the snow gave way, and he fell on the hard marble that was Sara's Tombstone. As it became known in the pubs when the truth came out, "the dead hit back."

Turns out that the dead hit very hard as he ended up tearing his ACL, MCL, LCL, and PCL in his right leg meaning that the strength speed and athleticism that were once his were completely gone. Most of the time a single one of those you can come back. A total knee tends to take away the strength and speed. For ball players like Theo, the only thing they have is speed and strength and the knowledge that nothing will go wrong. It leads to that cockyness, that was why he could run full speed into a wall of humanity, and that is what made him unstoppable. Now that was gone. He lost his scholarship and his future in one swift moment.

Now, that's Karma for you…

Chapter Ten
A Part Missing

"I need to show you something, but I think it might be really painful." Stephanie said suddenly as Johnny was wrapping his head with new bandages. The old ones were looking sickening with the dry blood cracking.

"What?" Johnny asked, wondering what more could come out of today.

"I can't really tell you, I have to show you. Will you promise not to get too mad about it?" She asked sounding real nervous. A very drastic turn from her normally bubbly attitude towards life.

"Yeah? What?" He said wondering what it could possibly be.

They went back through the women's locker room, and out into the hallway. From there they walked down the hall into the academic wing. Stephanie seemed nervous and jittery all the way, making Johnny jittery as well as he walked along by her.

"What is it?"

"Well I wondered if you remember that day where *I* was?"

"No, where were you?"

"Well I was down there. I remember rushing to the scene, I remember seeing you there. I remember seeing Sara. It still haunts me to that day. Sara was one of my best friends."

"You had to witness it too." Johnny said, thinking to himself that finally someone knew what he was going through.

"Yeah, I remembered running like crazy trying to help everyone out.

I think I was the one that called the ambulance and all. But anyway, the day of the funeral, I didn't go if you'll recall."

"I wouldn't know…I didn't get to go to it. You couldn't face it though?"

"Yeah. I went driving that afternoon, and I ended up back at the accident scene. You know how you end up places and you're not sure how you got there? Yeah that was me…anyway I was looking around and there was this rock, big thing…like five feet tall and a couple feet across." She said and she seemed to get teary, "and I got all shook up and went and sat down on it, and I remember thinking to myself, this was the last thing Sara saw…and then I looked down, and I found this camera."

"You found our camera?" Johnny asked shocked.

"Yeah…I did. I wanted to give it to you, I really did. But then I thought that it would hurt too much to have it. Anyway, I just got the courage up a while ago to do the film." She said as they entered the dark room.

She went over to a cabinet and pulled out a picture that was the size of a sheet of paper, and handed it in her shaking hands to Johnny. He picked it up and turned over.

In the red light that was the dark room, he took a look at the photo. It showed a smiling younger version of himself, with less scars less aging, with arm extended. To his right was Sara, wearing her bright red tee shirt, smiling with her head against his. In the background there was a cloudless blue sky, thundering majestic mountains and in the middle was a small infamous little strip of running water, Mystic Creek.

A glimpse of the future lying in the past….

He looked up at Stephanie with a lump in his throat. It was one of those looks that says everything that you wish you could say, everything that you can't say, everything that he felt, you could just see it in his eyes. One of those looks where you see it and you don't even want to know what it means. I know it sounds odd but there was so much love and hate in that stare that one look that you would think you were standing between Satin and God himself.

I guess sometimes you can't put to words what you feel…

It turns out that there were more pictures. Lots more pictures, every one of them a piece of treasured art to Johnny. It must have ripped him up something horrid to look at them knowing full well what happened hours later. But there was one photo that I am sure drove the acidic knife into his heart.

There was a picture that Sara had taken of herself inside the Ranger, right before the accident. We are talking so literally close in the period of time that if you looked in the distance you could see the car that Johnny and Sara were hit by. But she didn't look sad, she was smiling then.

What a way to go too...smiling in the face of death...

As much as it pained Johnny to look at he couldn't keep his eyes off it. It was something too special, too painful, too good to be true. I know that there will be those who say that there is no way that this camera could survive, that I am just making this up, but I guess it doesn't really matter. Whether or not the photo existed is irrelevant, whether Johnny saw it on a sheet of paper or in his mind's eye was just a matter of whether his eyes were open or not, because from that moment on he thought about nothing else.

Chapter Eleven
Philosophy and Chicken Fingers

Al Cheeseburgers was packed that afternoon. The only place open in town, all the local kids had gathered there that day for a little joke session, a place to eat and talk about everything that happened. When Johnny and Stephanie arrived the place was almost overflowing. Al was there serving out his usual cheese burgers, onion rings, French fries, malts, and every other thing that tastes so good that you can feel your arteries clog. I remember how Johnny walked in there with a big brown envelope, and he and Stephanie took a booth two seats away from the corner because while they weren't staring, everyone was noticing them. And I'm sure that there were rumors. But Johnny just shrugged them off.

"So are you mad at me?" Stephanie asked as Johnny stared at the pictures one by one as though he was analyzing them for a small detail.

"No…how can I be? I'm glad that at least someone had the chance to save these. It's almost like you saved her." He said with a smile of gratitude that I'm sure struck her as deep as she had struck him.

"If only saving a life could be done so easily." She protested biting into a chicken strip.

"You saved a memory for me that I thought I had lost. For the longest time I thought of that day with nothing but pain, but look at how happy she is there." He said tearing up. But he quickly withdrew his emotion. Not here…he thought, not in front of everyone. In typical style, he sucked up his emotions and became a shell again.

"Do you think that she knew?" Stephanie asked looking at the picture that was taken in her last moments wondering if she knew that was about to die. Johnny didn't say anything.

"In a sense I think she knew. I have always believed that we know when our time's up in the world. I think that she just wanted to enjoy every minute of it. Who knows maybe she's looking down from heaven right now?" She continued.

"I don't know, but a part of me wants her to be there doing that, a part of me wants her to be, but then again there's a part of me that doesn't want her to be watching. It sounds cruel, but a part of me wants the wound to heal and just get on with life you know?" Johnny said tentatively, not wanting to upset Stephanie on such a strong subject. He decided to hide inside his drink. But Stephanie wasn't looking to pick a fight.

"There's no shame in that."

"I don't know. I can't face it, though...truly letting her *go*. It's like a part of me was ripped out and now the wound is just sitting there bleeding out. A part of me wants to just go on living without that arm or leg, but I know it's hard so I keep trying to put it back in but it just never works you know?"

"Do you think the dead we love ever truly leave us?" Steph responded kindly and gently, "Sara is just as much a part of you now as she was only a few months ago. I can feel a part of her inside you, inside me, inside the very weave of the life this town lives upon. You see how much of a part of your life she becomes even though she has not truly been in it physically for months now."

"It's too hard to admit that she's gone. You don't think that she could be here, could she? I mean you said it yourself she is as much of a part of me as she ever was, what if her soul is right here and I can't touch it?"

"You can't touch it Johnny, because you still feel it." Stephanie said, taking a bite into her chicken strips, "you'll never come to terms with it until you accept that she isn't. Your hand is still holding on to her body, even though the rest of you has moved on."

Johnny looked away and looked around the packed restaurant. Everyone was sitting there laughing and smiling enjoying themselves. No one there truly felt, no one had anything that they were truly saying.

All there was, was chatter, blank words coming out of empty mouths.

Yet Johnny yearned to be like them. A part of him yearned to be just like the girl sitting on front of him. Not a care in the world, emotionally blocked from even the most powerful blows that life can deal out. I know for a fact that he did. I have to admit that it is one of the great ironies; all Johnny wanted to feel was the great nothingness of the inability to feel. That's why he cut, just so there was some sort of reason for the emotional pain. That's why he wrote; to siphon off some of the energy that was inside him. There was no denying it: he felt everything a guy can feel. But that's all that he needed, was just that ability to feel, that's all he hated was feeling.

That's it. When it comes to the end that's all Johnny had was feeling, and there is nothing he wanted less than the ability to feel.

"You haven't even been back there, have you?" Stephanie asked, dipping a French fry into some ketchup, "you haven't even been back to Mystic Creek. I bet you're just terrified of it."

Johnny gave her a look of almost hate almost truth, but he said nothing, Stephanie sensing this continued quickly, "there's no shame in that fear. The horrors you've experienced there, I can't imagine, but then again they have to come to fruition. All things have a cycle Johnny, and some day you will have to face that intersection again."

"Perhaps." Johnny suggested, "I don't know if I could go today, or even tomorrow. I need to go, but I know I can't go alone; I need you to come with me. Can you help me?"

"I think I can try, as long as you are willing to help yourself. Otherwise, it's just gonna cause you more pain, and I don't want to see that."

And thus the healing begins, like all wounds this one too would close up; the unfortunate part is that when it does, it ain't pretty.

Scars and scabs sometimes look worse than the wound itself.

Chapter Twelve
Opening the Wound

If I were a better liar, I'd tell you that Johnny wanted to go when Stephanie started up the engine to her Ford Excursion. If I were a lawyer, I would tell you that Johnny thought of all the times that he had taken that same trip with Sara, and how he had a small tear fall from his eye when they left Elysium. Fortunately, I am neither a liar nor a lawyer, I am a narrator; I deal with the truth that is in every lie. Truth be told I don't think Johnny even realized that they had arrived when the Excursion pulled to a halt. It's like arriving at a place and not exactly knowing how you got there, that's Johnny for you.

The intersection was small, a two lane street turning at a "T" to another two lane, following parallel along Mystic Creek, which flowed some ten feet below on the embankment smoothly on top but with a swift undercurrent. There was a sense of peace to people looking at it. A "small town feel" as some say. I personally don't know. I lost a lot there so it's hard for me to say with any accuracy.

Me, I remember Johnny getting out. There he saw the cross on the side of the road. It was half buried in the snow, but he could still see the name etched in black. He looked at the thing with fear and disgust. It wasn't even in the right place. If they wanted to put it where Sara had died, they should have placed it right dead smack in the cross-bound lane, he thought. The scene flashed in his mind's eye.

The ranger was turned over, the car was on fire. The other car, a black F350 was in shambles. Its engine was now in the passenger seat, the hood was completely ripped off. Its driver was ripped into two pieces when he got ejected out, Johnny had heard. Johnny didn't really care about that guy. As far as he was concerned there was no reason for sympathy for the man that caused this horror.

His judgment commeth...

I seem to remember that the man driving the other car was in a hurry to get home. He had been drinking but from the reports he was an alcoholic. But they have a hard time measuring your BAC when they wash what is left of you off the pavement. But don't you dare debase what happened there by blaming it on alcohol. It was the man driving in a hurry. He was going 67 MPH in a 35 area. He thought he could handle it.

I guess a lot of people think a lot of things...

Johnny walked through the snow to the cross and knelt down. As he did he could see the car, he could see the accident all over again. No matter how hard he tried to escape it he couldn't. The silent screams all over again.

He was standing there pulling as hard as he could, but the door wouldn't budge. When it finally did, he pulled it away and there was Sara. Limp and bloody, but then again so was he as far as blood goes. Johnny didn't really have to think. He unbuckled her while pleading under her breath, "please God let her be alright...please God..."

*I guess there really isn't any such thing as an atheist in a fox hole...*Johnny thought. He didn't like the idea of a Heaven. He didn't like the idea of life as a test. There was too much things that said otherwise in this world. Like why do people fight so hard to stay alive if there is this great place we go to when we die? Why live in misery if we live eternally in something that's wonderful?

He saw the cross that had been laid where Sara had apparently been killed. The way he remembers it, he was right in the middle of that god-forsaken intersection when he pulled her from that car. Why he didn't get her out earlier is anyone's guess.

I'm no psychologist but I think that is one of the reasons that Johnny blamed himself for her death. I remember telling you that he got out of the car, and the question becomes why didn't he see her and pull her out with him.

The answer: he had one hell of a wreck. He was inside a giant piece of twisted metal that had started on fire when he first realized it. The memory of the wreck was so horrid and vivid that for a while he just blanked it out. It kind of hard to explain, but his mind just couldn't take it, seeing it again. He blacked it from his memory, the entire day's trip. I imagine that all he could bear to handle is that Sara was with him when she died.

The water on Mystic Creek was far from running as it had been that day. The entire little stream that flowed through the little town was completely frozen over. If Johnny had wanted to he could have walked over the snow covering the ice from one side to the other.

"What are you doing Johnny?" Stephanie asked as he found himself walking towards the water.

"I...just-you know have to do something." Johnny muttered lamely.

I have to imagine Stephanie understood looking at him as he slipped and slide down the wet slope through the snow right towards Mystic Creek. There was something entrancing about it. He reached the spot where the ice had grown thick and he walked out on the frozen water about halfway across and looked up into the sky. He closed his eyes and took everything in, at least once again. The smell of the pine and the snow and the feel of the water. I know it sounds idiotic, but Johnny could feel the slow push of the water underneath his feet, the way that it moved forward, the way that no matter how everything tried to stop it and freeze it into place. Johnny just sat there breathing it all in, the flashes the pain the guilt the love, the loss, everything just swirling. But unlike the other times, this time, it felt good.

He then walked up to where the cross was hammered into the frozen ground. There were many people's notes written on it in sharpie markers, and a long the cross there was Sara's name. It was white like the snow around it, and Johnny quickly brushed away the snow while holding back tears.

He then reached into his pocket where he picked up a small razor and took a quick slice at his forearm. The pain felt good to him, as it kept him off the pain he was feeling emotionally. He then pinched closed the wound, and dripped some of the blood on to the base of the small cross, along with it was a tear.

"In blood and tears, I shed me this pain. For the last time, shed in your name." He rhymed slowly under his breath.

I'm not sure whether Stephanie heard this part of Johnny's little ritual or not, but I don't think that's really all that important. For him there was a certain sense of having done something productive, something right, something that for the first time would mean something to him. Yes it was not the thing that most people would do but it was what Johnny needed to have done.

The scab would soon heal, and with it, I think we all hope, would be his heart.

Chapter Thirteen
Picking and Choosing

Now I don't really want to talk much more about what Johnny did at Mystic Creek, because that was what he needed to heal and in some senses we all need something different to heal. The ride back for him was a little bit easier than the rest of the day had been. I think it was about that time that he started to feel just a little better, he started to feel just a little more like he was alive. But whenever something like that happens, something goes wrong. Johnny knew it was coming, he just didn't figure that it would be something like what ended up happing.

Everyone talks about bringing those who have lost someone "closure" as though it really helps that much. Johnny had in some senses returned to closure, and he was starting to heal for the first time in months. I imagine a little smirk on his face as he rode in the passenger seat of Stephanie's SUV, though I really don't know for sure. He would turn on the radio and for a fleeting moment I see him feeling as though he too was free. It's like a flash back for him, and unfortunately this happiness would be short lived.

On the way back, for whatever reason Stephanie decided to pull into Sara's old house. And Johnny started to get a bit more nervous. Whenever he went by this place, he felt the sudden rush associated with the silent screams he had by night.

"What are we doing here?" He asked.

"Well, I think if anyone deserves to have these pictures, it's Sara's parents. It's all that they will ever have of their daughter." Stephanie explained. Johnny felt almost betrayed.

"You realize her mom wants me dead. She blames me for her death." Johnny said as they walked up to the door. He had hoped there would be some part of Stephanie that realized this but it was to no avail.

Stephanie rang the doorbell; I guess there was no turning back from there...

"Stephanie!" Sara's mom exclaimed coming to the door, and then upon seeing Johnny muttered, "and *you*."

"I know things are going bad for you ma'm, but there's something we think that you should see." Stephanie said somewhat like the cop that had explained to Sara's mother that her daughter was dead.

"What are these?" She asked opening the envelope ignoring the sudden jolt from the bad memory.

"These are from *that* day. The day that your daughter died." Johnny said slightly shook up.

"I don't believe it. You slimy piece of shit...you think that I'm supposed to feel sorry for you?" she said shaking her head in disbelief.

"No," Johnny interjected, "I know that you have no room in your heart to feel any sympathy towards me. There's not a day that goes by that I don't cry over what happened to her."

"Good." Sara's mom said venomously.

"Ma'm, I know you never liked me. I know that no matter how much I wish it were different, Sara is dead. But I think that you should know that I know about Sara's Cancer. She didn't have as much time left as you think that I robbed her of."

"How do you know that?" She screamed, "They said there was a chance of survival. She could've been normal!"

"We'll never know one way or the other. She could have lived Lord knows how many days more. Funny thing about cancer is that it doesn't tend to follow a set path. It kind of jumps you in the back ally and then leaves you to suffer. So, if you can think yourself righteous telling yourself that you would have saved her, then go right ahead. I know that it wouldn't have been that great of a life, losing all your hair from Chemo, sitting there in a hospital bed day and night, wondering why in the hell you're fighting so hard to keep holding on if where you're going is so wonderful…That's not living, that's prolonging the inevitable."

Sara's mom gave him a back handed slap right to the face. It was a good dirty slap and it twisted Johnny's neck violently and tore open one of the scars on his face. He spun to gain his balance as he staggered down the steps. He then spat out some blood out of his mouth, and then looked with a great pity at the woman in front of him.

"You know what the last words your daughter ever said were? No? She said and I quote, 'I feel so good right now, I could die…*and be happy.*' Half a second later a car driven by a drunk driver slammed into the side of my car and I was the only one that survived. So live in your hate if it makes you feel better, but I for one am going to try and heal. I think that if Sara could have chosen, that is what she would have chosen." He said.

"Thanks to you we'll never know."

"I know, but that doesn't mean anything. I think that I can live for the rest of my life knowing that when Sara went, she was at least happy. These should be enough proof to show any person alive that she is resting in peace, but if you want, go ahead, keep believing that I'm the problem here. Come and shoot me in the middle of the night, but the only thing that will return your daughter to you is to honor the memory of the person she was."

"I can never forgive you…but she might have been able to." Sara's mother said sensing a small amount of defeat, pulling a small envelope out of seemingly nowhere, "She was going to send this to you after we started her treatment at the Mayo Clinic in Minnesota. But that never happened…"

Johnny took the envelope that had not been opened and put it in his pocket of his sweatshirt and walked out into the driveway. The letter was written in Sara's handwriting with his address and no return address…

"I can't open it…" He said as Stephanie walked closer. She took it into her hands and carefully took out an aged piece of paper.

"I'll read it…." Johnny said his heart racing. The page was written on a simple piece of notebook paper in a black pen.

Dear John,

Were it that I was as gifted with words as you are, so that maybe the terrible burden I am to bestow upon you could somehow be lessened, that somehow I could write words that didn't cut as deep of wounds, but such is not the way of the pen. May it be that when you read this, you find some understanding and that in some way shape or form, you may find peace. It is my last wish that you find peace, that you find hope, that you remember love.

I was diagnosed with a terminal strain of cancer. They don't know what caused the cancer, but they are sure that I won't make it much longer in much the same way that doctors can be certain. Though I do not accept their judgment, I know my time is drawing to a close, and this shall be the last time that you will hear from me. Oh were it so easy that they would only know that which causes these things…they say that they have a treatment at the Mayo Clinic, but I know better than to believe that I will ever see the mountains again. In a certain respect a part of me wishes that my soul may leave here, that my soul may return to God's grace in the part of this world that he has left us to remember that he is here. Twere it so easy that I could leave my body, and let dust become dust once again, whilst I feel love, while I still have the mindset of peace. Were it that I could fall asleep in your arms tonight and never wake up…

I must leave John, and that is the simple fact of life. Were it so easy, that I would be able to tell you this in person but I can't, I never could and that is the only truth that drives this pen across paper. I never had the courage that you will need to have, for you must live on John. You must live the dream that I can no longer. You must be the one who carries on. I know that many tears will be shed, but know that I don't wish for any of them. It is my hope that in this way that you might perceive my death in the same way that I could make it if I in control of such things. I wish that that you would live on as though I have merely moved away. I hope that you will someday tell our story, tell it in the way that only you could.

I hope that you will someday go before the oceans, and speak out the truth that they are.

Early natives once said that the Pacific Ocean has no memory. I hope that you find your way there some time, that you can know a place that can't remember where you are. I hope that you find yourself there.

I loved you John, more than anything. You were everything that a woman could ask for. You made the short amount of time that I had left something worth living for. You must now be the voice that I no longer have. You must be my eyes, and my soul. For I live on in you... In some senses I am not really gone. If you loose your faith in me, my love, never loose your faith in people. I know that out there is a mystery, and that we are to find the joy in not knowing it. Regardless of the reason, things happen, and they therefore have reason. I wish that I had a better explanation to give you, but I don't, and I can't take much more.

I never really thought that I would ever really say this, but Goodbye Johnny, I love you so much. I love you so much Johnny, and I know that you will always love me. I will never forget you my love, for you have made this a life complete.

Forever yours, our love lives eternal,
My best hopes and wishes to you my love,
~Sara~

It felt like hours later when Stephanie joined him in the car, and they then drove out to the cemetery that he had tried to go to earlier. He got out of the car alone; he took out one of the pictures. It was of him and Sara.

The picture was a regular 4x6, but it was one that he knew that he would never forget. Out of the picture, Sara's eyes stared straight at him, a small mischievous smile on her face, as though she knew how Johnny would feel in the future...the concoction of pain and happiness, or sorrowful bliss, or embraceful release into the world. Johnny could almost feel her presence as he looked around. The sun shining bright off the fresh fallen snow, the grandness of it all. He tried to take it all in. He wasn't letting her go, he decided, he was meeting back with her.

Finally Free...

That's all he said along with, "Rest in peace Sara. You will never be forgotten."

Chapter Fourteen
The Shadow of the Man

There is a lot of tales of this day. The one that no one really knows, or at least the one that you will hear the least is that of what happened to Theo Sandburg. The tale that he tells everyone is that he was up there paying his respects and that something twisted inside his knee.

Theo had a complete knee reconstruction that month. He had more iron than flesh in his knee and try as he might, the damage was significant enough to where he knew that he would never get to play football again. He became addicted to Vicodin from what I remember. Either that or OxyCodine, either way when those ran out and the doctor's wouldn't give him more he turned to Heroin. Everything fell apart for him that day. He never told anyone why it was that he was up there or how it was that he was injured. Hell he went around ranting at all of his friends at how pissed he was that he spent about an hour in shock from what happened and half buried in snow.

The truth with Theo is that he will never get to be a player in college and that he never will walk right again. I remember how he ended up in jail for a couple months then out, really it's been fun to watch in the papers because at first there was a chance that Theo would have been able to get to maybe play at a Junior College, or perhaps even Division III, but no one wanted to take a chance on someone who would likely not turn out and had a serious drug problem. Johnny wouldn't have liked it as much if he hadn't known what really happened to Theo. Johnny was able to think up some highly poetic justice, and that gave him some satisfaction.

As for Stephanie, she went on to become a nurse in upper California. She kept in touch with Johnny briefly out of high school but that was before he began traveling the world. She still paid her respects yearly as always but was not heard much from those in Elysium. Legend has it that she was the one that created a very small memorial that appeared one morning on the shore of Mystic Creek. It was a large pewter heart that was engraved with the phrase, "though at long last I see that the Heaven I sought lay before me all along, and I learned that the journey begins at the end." To this day it still is there, though rather weathered from its location.

I think that a part of Johnny would have loved to know that he was not going to be remembered for very long in Elysium. There were few that were sorry to see the back of him, but they faded in time. After a while no one really knew the story of Johnny and Sara. As with most of history the truth fades into legend, and the legend is replaced by new truths in the years to come. There are a few that still remember the story, but they are few and far between. After about a year or so there was almost no one there that knew where Johnny had gone.

But to Johnny that didn't really matter. The point to him was that he was gone and that was all that mattered to him.

Chapter Fifteen
Pages Go Blank Forever

Writing. That's how this story began, Johnny writing, and the pages I can tell you look a lot different. For one thing the original ending to the book he was writing was with the young Queen committing suicide after realizing that there was nothing left in the world to live for after the loss of her only child. It's a sad ending, but it's the truth and that matters more than any sentiment ever could. The truth is a powerful force in this universe. And in this case the truth takes far more precedence than sentiment.

Johnny ended that day writing. It was different though, something inside him was driving the pencil foreword across the page. Something inside him had changed. He kept that picture out in front him as he wrote. Having written for years, he never felt the writers' cramp and the end of the play was coming up. As it so happens it would become one of his high school's best performed pieces and Johnny was right there in the front row when it was performed. I have to imagine that he saw it all before it actually happened, because it felt so real, so wonderfully done. It starts with the Queen looking out the window as her faithful friend Bartholomew looks on.

Bartholomew:

"What hath changed, my Lady? T'was not an hour past that I thought you touched for the rest of life, yet I see thee now the lady I once knew, Queen Aras of Delthamar."

Queen:

"A change, Bartholomew? So much has changed. But I realize now that as I move forward, my heart remains with them so in actuality I have not left them, but I shall not be imprisoned there in the darkest corner of my mind."

Bartholomew:

"T'was cruel my Lady…thou knowest that my sympathies…" (Cut off)

Queen:

"Cruel Bartholomew? I took thee for a better man… T'was not cruelty nor wrath but the Reaper that came that day. But he is the Sheppard Angel of the Lord, and T'was he that did take my love away…"

~Johnny~

That night I seem to remember, that Johnny had his final visit from Sara. They were back at the scene of the accident, but without the wreck, without the pain, Sara was there wearing a robe of dazzling white, a heavenly aura around her, though she didn't have any wings or a halo.

"Still writing as ever…" She said coming out of nowhere while Johnny was writing on the banks of Mystic Creek.

"I actually have decided, Sara. The pages go blank forever now. There will be no more writing Sara. I can't let myself do this anymore. I am opening wounds that will never close if I don't stop."

Sara smiled at him, walking into the water slowly surrounding herself in the soft flow of the waves…

"What you chase in writing is the same thing that you chase in life my love, that's a way to set yourself free."

"That may be true. But the thing is, one I can attain and the other I can't. That's why I have to stop writing."

"Promise me one thing, Johnny." Sara said wadding out into the water, Johnny just watched silently.

"What's that?"

"Your last book. Tell our story. I want you to tell the story so that people will know when they read it what it was really like."

"I think that I can do that." Johnny said, taking her hand, and he then kissed her.

She hung her arms around his shoulders, and from there, she walked with him forward towards a light.

At the Water's End

"Es triste senor...so sad, this book you wrote..." The Bartender responded as the man closed the book.

The night was hitting the bay and the bar was fluttering with its usual locals and travelers from so many areas across the world. By this time there were many listeners, but most of them weren't really showing they were listening, yet many of them were touched by what they had heard in the story that had started at the bar.

The sunset was now almost over, the sky was black, dark orange, and red. The waves were calmer now, versus the surfing that had been going on all day outside the bay where the small bar lay on the coarse sand. It was almost as though mother nature herself had been listening to the entire story and she too laid to rest; the bright passionate sun slipping low into the bottomless sea and abyss that lay below.

"So that's supposed to be the truth of what happened? I don't remember anything like that ever happening." The publicist said mildly annoyed with his prodigy writer.

"It's the truth, or as close as anyone is going to come to it...It's what I can remember, and it's all I need. Because in truth what I seek won't set me free, for what I know now is that I am to seek the happiness that I can never find. Think about it George. You will someday understand what it means and until then take this." He said handing him the book as well as the empty bottle of gin.

"He is you, isn't he? This Johnny..."

"I suppose..." The man responded with a small laugh putting out the

79

last bit of a Cuban cigar that he had lit during his reading, "but then again, he's in a lot of people. There's a truth to what happened to Johnny, but if you'll excuse me, I have to get going. There's one last thing that I have to do."

The tall dark man walked out of the bar alone as the night life was starting to get going. As he walked around the town he noticed how the people there seemed to be all enjoying themselves. He didn't like the confliction of feelings. He hadn't liked it for so many years and for a long while he knew that there wasn't anything that he could do about that. But this was different. He almost could feel the certainty to the situation.

The sand was smooth under his feet as he kicked off his sandals and then his shirt. He walked about a mile to a bluff that extended strait out into the ocean about fifty feet above the shallow water. He sat alone in the moonlight for a couple minutes before he stood at the edge taking in the beauty of the scenery. He then opened up his heart and with a swooping sensation he closed his eyes and completed the task he had set out to do.

"Not in cruelty nor in wrath did the reaper come today…Sheppard angel of the Lord please take my soul away…" He whispered out into the night before he fell but the night responded back and he was at the top of the bluff again.

"Leave it to a writer to never do anything without an overtly poetic and highly plagiarized speech." Came a familiar voice that he had not heard in years.

In the void of the night a bright white light emerged and out of the rip in space and time came a young beautiful woman just the way that he had remembered her.

"Sara…" He said before he ran up to embrace her. She felt just the same as he had remembered…so warm so full as though each and every hole in his soul was somehow filled and complete in purpose and meaning…something now completely pure. He was finally completely whole.

"John…It's been so long, but it feels just the way that I remembered it…I thought you would come here tonight." She said overjoyed at what she was seeing her smile seemed just as alive and vibrant as it had been the last time that Johnny had seen her.

"Why didn't you stop me, like you did in the past?" Johnny asked as he let go of the embrace.

"You had purpose tonight. The story lives on…That mattered. It means that neither of us were to have died in vain, and frankly what was to stop you?" She said giving him a kiss as they stood on the edge in the moonlight as the waves slowly crashed on the rocks so far below them. It felt distant, and serene. It was as though it was programmed background music. *The hymnal of the sea.…*

"You knew…I'm sorry Sara, but I couldn't be anything without you. I pissed away all my money, I chased off every person that ever loved me. Lately I can't find any way to live in a world that seems so empty and alone. So I wrote the last I knew and I came here, for it was your last wish." He said and surprisingly he felt no guilt for his actions though he knew that his words showed it.

"You wrote the story I could never tell. I think it was better for you to join me here. So here's to the greatest welcome back that I've ever had."

Sara then kissed Johnny and he felt as though he was alive in every sense of the word. He became happy and content for the first time in years and the scars seemed to fade away. There for the first time in many, many, years stood the shadow of the light, what Johnny had always been.

"Do you think they'll ever find it?" Sara said looking over the edge where the lifeless remnants crashed against the rocks, slowly heading out with the fading tide; out to the abyss of the Pacific Ocean.

"I hope not. I think it'll finally be at peace, or at least I hope that the sea swallows it into the abyss and hides the darkness from this world…" Johnny said, looking out at the deep ocean, "You once told me that the Water called…I guess to me the water now calls. My debt to be paid for the sins that I can't forgive myself for…"

"That's neither here nor there…*We* are neither here nor there. I think that I'll enjoy spending the rest of the Eternity with you." Sara said her arm around Johnny's shoulder. Once again he felt whole and complete.

There was something about Sara's embrace that was as full in spirit as Johnny could imagine.

The winds blew off the ocean and Johnny closed his eyes and he was sitting back on the giant log that went over the top of Mystic Creek. The winds blew calmly at their backs. Johnny and Sara sat calmly letting the cool waters from the mountain top flow silently lapping at their feet.

"Paradise…it kind of has a new meaning, besides who needs bright lights and glory? I have you." Johnny said and for the first time Heaven meant something more than what he had read about it.

"I should apologize. We could have both had exactly that. When it all happened…I was given a choice. I chose to watch over you…and at one point it looked like they were going to loose you on the way to the hospital and I stepped in."

"Stepped in?"

"John, you were inches from death, and I realize that I should have let you die. I prolonged it. I breathed life into you and let you live. I didn't realize that it would come to this." She said with her head drooping in.

"This?" Johnny said looking around, "it may be that I am to remain here for all eternity. With you, what more could I ask for?"

"I just want you to know. You could have been so much more. I was meant to die that day. It is the way life goes that I wasn't going to survive very long. I didn't realize that you would be affected so greatly." She said with a bit of sadness in her eyes.

"*You* should have been so much more." Johnny said putting his arms around his beautiful girl.

"I was. Through you. It's quite interesting that you and I end up back here. It's so peaceful…so beautiful. The natives once spoke of spirits that ran through these woods, chasing each other along this river. That was how they named this place."

"I hate to point out the obvious, but I think that they were talking about us." He said with a smile, looking around at the primitive Eden that they were in. It was a prospect unlike any other that he was used to.

"It's kind of fitting isn't it? They name the spirits after us, we meet there, we love there, and then we die there, and as we are resurrected we go back. A circle complete…"

"I guess that's why they chose to call it Mystic Creek."